Gareth Clarke

SENSIBILITY PLUS

HZPublishing

Copyright © 2020 by Gareth Clarke

All rights reserved. No part of this book may be reproduced or used in any manner without written permission of the copyright owner except for the use of quotations in a book review. For more information, address: garethclarke137@gmail.com

HZPublishing

Sensibility Plus

'You see, we are not accustomed to horrible ideas…we haven't any.'

Herland - Charlotte Perkins Gilman

1

Hugo had what Pippa called finely chiselled features. She also often remarked upon his flared nostrils, tall dark smouldering looks, bedroom eyes and sensuous lips. But then Pippa was something quite important in publishing. Commissioning editor for an obscure but moderately successful London-based publishing house. And too much romcom must inevitably play havoc with one's judgement. Daily immersion in chick lit and green and pink flowery covers, with or without embossed lettering, must inevitably erode one's sense of well-being, to the extent that the depth of one's superficiality must often be forced to plumb uncharted shallows. But she made the best of an overpaid job, and brought much that was unreadable before the eyes of many tens of thousands of gentle readers.

Monday morning in the conference suite, in fact a fairly poky square room with table and chairs squeezed against the wall around it. And Sally, literary editor at the Freddy Thomson Publishing Co. Ltd, friend and protégé of Pippa, was on the rampage. The trend and tenor of her sustained rant was all too familiar to all the Rebeccas, Pippas, Aramintas, Felicitys, Jemimas and Daniels hemmed in around the table, pens in hands, creative juices primed and ready to freely flow. And the peculiar object of her objectivity was the imminent debut novel of one Sophie or Rosie or Georgina, at any rate some old university chum of Pippa's, and herself coincidentally ensconced in publishing, journalism, PR or other closely related activity.

'They are all interchangeable. The characters have no separate identity. The characters are not characters at all in the sense of having any distinct character. They are, in fact, identikit cut-outs. There is no consistency to the characterisation in this novel. Where there is consistency to the characterisation it is because the characters are not characters in the first place, but merely caricatures of types that never had any definable character in the first place. They simply conform to a more or less rigid template of what a character of that particular specification would have said in any given and entirely predictable situation in any one of the trillion or so similar works. In short, this novel, conforming as it does to precisely the same format regarding the non-characters, predictable plotting, careworn settings, and dire dialogue of its interminable predecessors, is tripe. It should never be published. Ever.'

There was silence from the open mouths ranged around the table. That is apart from several loud sniffs from Jemima, editor of the stuff broadly lumped together as romcom and chick lit, and who had therefore been responsible for promoting the novel under discussion.

Even by Sally's standards, her attack was strong stuff. Especially as the author of this tripe, be it Georgina, Rosie or Sophie, was one of Pippa's oldest friends. But it was entirely typical of Sally's determination to stay true to her own exalted standards, regardless of consequences.

There was an embarrassed exchange of looks, and a degree of uncertainty as to whether hysterical laughter would be in order. That was it, of course! It was a joke! Sally's idiosyncratic sense of humour! That's why she'd been taken on in the first place, for just that unique left-field take on matters.

'Don't you think you're exaggerating more than somewhat, Sally?' said Pippa, with a smile and a kind, encouraging expression.

'No, I don't. It is not merely tripe - it is superannuated, super-tripe! And it's surely, surely time we pensioned this loathsome sub-genre and its whole nauseating substratum of practitioners to some remote, dusty shelf of well-merited obscurity.'

Okay - seemed to be the consensus - maybe she wasn't joking. Maybe, in fact, she meant every word.

'Look, Sally, if you feel this strongly about it maybe we should refer it to Freddy before going ahead with the contract. For me, personally, it ticks all the boxes, but we need some measure of agreement before pushing ahead. I'm always reluctant to do so if someone has strongly negative feelings about a piece.'

'Freddy!' cried Sally with an incredulous expression. 'Poor old Freddy! That walking non sequitur! You're not really going to ask his opinion, are you?'

A few nervous giggles around the table.

'Darling, he is the MD. He did found this firm. We wouldn't be sitting round this table now if he hadn't.'

'Maybe we'd be sitting in a little more comfort if he was better at his job, and if the firm was more successful and more discriminating. I can hardly bloody breathe stuck against the wall here! Look, I don't know how Freddy got involved in publishing, I really don't. Well, yes I do. To him, as to so many working in this so-called profession it's all about packaging tripe in a pretty container, with all the correct pastel shades' - superb derision in her tone - 'then selling it like soap powder. If we're just part of the retail sector, for God's sake let's do the job properly and start selling tins of beans and toilet rolls. At least they serve some useful purpose, unlike the tripe we sell.'

'I hate it when you talk about our work like this,' said Araminta, an amply proportioned, immaculately presented young lady with long, dark hair and a powerful, flowery perfume. 'It undermines everything we do here and all the work and all the writers we try to support.'

Her expression was one of indignant affront, and her rebuke was accompanied by a glance tacitly inviting the support of Pippa. Sally's pretty lip curled in scorn.

'Don't try too hard, Minty! You might strain something. I never read the rubbish you like, anyway. Thrillers and sex crimes - that's tripe by definition. Unpleasant tripe, what's more, that does nothing for human nature but legitimise its worst aspects.'

'That's a very tired and very old argument, Sally. And I know for a fact that Freddy regards the genre as an important and central part of what we sell.'

'Buy 2 for the price of 1! 50% off while stocks last! Reduced to clear! Damaged stock - must unload onto any credulous moron that will buy it!

Maybe you're fast approaching your sell-by date, Minty. Or is it best before?'

'Sally, please,' said Pippa. 'Let's try to keep this discussion constructive. Please. There's no place here for personal attacks. I think you owe Araminta an apology.'

Sally smiled innocently across the table towards Araminta's sour and red-hued face.

'Sorry, Minty, I think all the tripe you offload onto an unsuspecting public is simply wonderful. And I'm sure Freddy thinks the world of you, and values your work above anyone else's. And his judgement is usually so sound. He is, after all, one of those rare individuals who never fails to fall victim to the magnitude of the occasion. He never hesitates to stoop to conquer the giddy heights of his own ineptitude. In fact,' continued Sally, warming to her task, 'you could say his gifts are transparently oblivious. In fact, his extraordinary lack of talent is only the least of his recommendations. In many other respects, his obscurity precedes him.'

'You're being very unkind,' said Pippa, endeavouring to conceal her amusement.

'I'm being clinically precise. Which may or may not amount to the same thing. And the only reason stuff like this' - picking up the manuscript, then dropping it again with a dramatic thump on the table - 'needs so much editing (thanks to my wonderful editor Clare or Vicky or Helen or Amanda - you know who you are - for all your belief, care, patience, expertise and generally holding my tits during the whole period of creation of this piece of tripe), is because they're no bloody good in the first place!'

'Every writer needs an editor, Sally.'

'These people aren't writers - they're criminals, guilty of a swathe of offences against the English language, crimes against the imagination, vicious attacks against the taste and capacity for suspension of intellect of any even halfway intelligent reader.'

'Do we have to listen to any more of this completely non-constructive kind of comment,' said Araminta, her face now crimson with indignation. 'If Sally doesn't like writers or the publishing profession, perhaps she's chosen the wrong career path.'

'And maybe you've chosen the wrong bra size, Minty, and that's why you're looking so uncomfortable. Why don't you just go and…read a beginner's guide to ethics.'

Minty's lips quivered, and she appeared on the verge of tears. Jemima looked ready to take things one step further, now sniffling into a tissue.

'Ladies, ladies. Please.'

Pippa massaged her forehead. Twice during this noisy and combative meeting she'd heard the familiar bleeping of a received text. Tentatively she'd reached down to her bag and felt her fingers close around Hugo's mobile, which that morning she'd taken and concealed, pretending to be busy while Hugo raced round searching and swearing, his agitation in stark contrast to his customary laid-back manner. Twice during the meeting she'd felt its cold, hard shape, but then released her hold out of nothing less than fear, unable to make herself draw the phone from her bag.

And then there was the guilt. Both for the deception, and also for the doubts that had prompted it. Her naturally calm, mature and gentle self-possession reduced to subterfuge and disloyalty. And yet what choice did she have? Hugo's behaviour over the past few weeks, usually kind and calm, amusing and consoling her with his dry, gentle wit, had been strangely elliptical and preoccupied. It was all so uncharacteristic. Such that she simply had to know the reason, one way or another.

'I have to say, that as far as this particular novel is concerned, I agree with Sally.'

Pippa looked up in surprise, though in fact it was no great surprise that Daniel had agreed with Sally. Men tended to agree with Sally on principle, the principle being that she was young, petite, shapely, exceptionally pretty and charismatically opinionated, and that there was therefore a kind of imperative in trying one's luck, however hopeless and foredoomed the attempt.

And Daniel was particularly well-placed to inspire Sally's absolute disregard. Late thirties, ginger hair, glasses, sideburns, green open-neck shirt. Probably hopelessly in love with Sally, as many were. Hopeless romantically, and also in terms of professional capability. Sally certainly viewed the firm's sedentary fortunes as due, at least in part, to Daniel's marginal marketing skills. But his unwavering support for her in meetings played against her contempt. And though usually immune to flattery, also stayed her tongue. Pity no doubt played some part.

'I don't mean this in any way as a reflection on Jemima, but I think it's a very weak example of what is, indeed, becoming an all too formulaic genre. I tend to agree with Sally that we need to be more discriminating in this area, or else there's a danger that our titles will be seen as little better than pulp fiction.'

At this Jemima, who'd been snuffling at progressively increasing levels of audibility, burst into floods of tears, and fled the room.

'There she goes!' said Sally. 'You can set your watch by her.'

'I'd better go after her,' said Daniel. 'I didn't mean to upset her.'

He followed Jemima out of the room.

'There's something going on there,' said Sally. 'Have you noticed how protective he is of her. And how often she has her eyes on him. I foresee the blossoming of true love! Their mutual lack of taste and perception will provide the sure foundation for a lifetime of exquisite connubial misunderstanding. She will live out her threadbare dreams through a romantic haze of stilted prose and shallow characterisation. He'll be her knight in green polyester, and they'll have two or three adorable children, who from an unfeasibly early age will lisp, I lub you mummy, and they'll all live happily ever after in a modernised terrace box in Richmond. What more could one wish for two such almost adequate individuals.'

'What gives you the right to judge everybody and everything?' burst out Araminta.

'Oh, slacken your straps, Minty! It's got nothing to do with you, anyway.'

'Look,' said Pippa, with a tired, preoccupied expression, 'I don't think we're going to get any further with this issue today. I'll have a word with Freddy and ask him to have a look over My Big

Secret! And I'll have another look at it myself. If I do pick up on any major, structural problems that I didn't see first time then, well okay, we'll think again. But if it's just a matter of style and personal taste then I still think we should press ahead. We know from experience it's the kind of book that will sell. And we do have to be able to sell the books we publish. And you know as well as I do, Sally, that what you call the tripe makes the modest profits that support and effectively underwrite the literary work that you value.'

'I'm just saying we should be more discriminating. I'm not saying we should stop selling tripe altogether, desirable though that would be. Just that it should be a better, more upmarket class of tripe, with dialogue just a shade more believable, plots a little more realistic, and clichés less shamelessly employed and liberally sprinkled.'

'Well, let's leave it at that, shall we. Araminta, do you think you could spare me a few minutes? If you could just pop into my office in, say, five minutes?'

Araminta had been carefully manoeuvring herself into open space during these last exchanges. With a disdainful sideways glance at Sally, she now swept from the room, trailing clouds of Dior.

'Christ!' said Sally, as the door closed behind her. 'What does that woman put on herself?'

'I do wish you'd try to be a little kinder and more diplomatic with Araminta, Sally. It would make life a lot easier.'

'It's always best to be upfront about things, Pippa. I think it's best that people know where they stand. So many problems in life stem from one person not having the slightest idea of what another is really thinking. And I think if you feel strongly about something, you should express your feelings openly. Anyway, I don't try to upset people. I don't mean to.'

'I know you don't, darling. And you're probably right. But being blunt and telling people exactly what I think is something I find particularly difficult.'

'I know you do,' said Sally kindly. 'Never mind, keep trying.'

2

Hugo, Pippa's husband, had always been a Porsche man, in every sense of the word. He'd stuck by the marque through thick and thin, from GT3 to Turbo, from Targa to Carrera. He worked in the city, for his sins, in investment banking. What exactly that entails I naturally prefer not to speculate, but doubtless it pays the bills.

Apart from the tall, chiselled, flared, smouldering, sensuous good looks, Hugo also had the good fortune to have someone in the office with whom he could pass the time of day, and talk the sort of men talk which, to women's mingled delight, derision and despair, men always do when gathered in small groups. Cars, sport, women's breasts. And occasionally women themselves - their blatant and universal insanity, and very often downright unpleasantness.

And cars it was that occupied their attention on this particular morning. Hugo's friend, surprisingly, was called Simon, and though less finely chiselled, smouldering or well-equipped in the bedroom eyes department, was nevertheless a presentable young man of, shall we say, twenty eight. Hugo threw the latest edition of Top Gear magazine onto Simon's desk, where it landed with a laddish thunk, scattering various pieces of paper which soared and spiralled in the sterile environment.

'What do you think of the S-Class?'

'Seriously? I always took you for a Porsche man, in every sense.'

'It's Pippa. Says we need something more practical. In case of eventualities.'

Simon grinned.

'Well, well! We're not going to hear the patter of tiny feet, are we?'

'Steady. Keep it clean. Of course not. Pippa's far too busy for anything like that.'

'But she wouldn't have to do anything. Apart from actually have the kid. Nobody looks after their own offspring these days. The professional classes don't consider it polite. It offends their sense of decency.'

He picked up a sheet of paper from the floor, crumpled it into a ball. Then using a fountain pen flicked it into a waste paper bin.

'Ha!'

'I hope that wasn't something important.'

'Oh, just some vital proposal or other.'

'Well, anyway, Pippa says a 4x4 is indispensable these days to cope with the hostile environment of Hampstead. So I thought I'd suggest the S-class, and hope she wouldn't notice that only two wheels are driven.'

'Women rarely pay attention to the number of wheels that are driven, except in an abstract sense.'

'That's what I thought. But the thing is, has the Stig tried it? I would never buy any car undriven by the Stig.'

'Very wise.'

'Who do you suppose he is, this Stig?'

'Oh, some failed racing driver or other, I dare say.'

'Perhaps it really is Stig,' said Hugo quietly. 'The real Stig.'

'What do you mean?'

'You know - Stig Blomquist, the great Swedish rally driver.'

'How Swedish was he?'

Hugo looked unsurprised.

'As Swedish as they come, so far as I know. Why do you ask?'

'It's just that many people claim to be Swedish for various reasons. And then of course it often turns out that they're not quite as Swedish as they'd been leading people to believe, leading to disappointment all round.'

'The things people do to attract attention.'

'Quite. And I can't really see the point, anyway. The Swedes are not the most charismatic of people

- apart from Abba and Per Eklund, of course. In fact, they're quite a taciturn race, much given to morbid reflection. And as I always say, if you have to indulge in reflection, for Heaven's sake don't do it morbidly. It shows on your face after only a few months. Years even, sometimes.'

He walked moodily to the window and gazed out at the commercial hub of the City. The buildings, all offices, were tall and shiny. And though they certainly possessed windows - equally shiny and opaque - it was impossible to conceive of intelligent, thinking, feeling beings existing behind them. And if there were such beings, existence was all that could be hoped for them amid such soulless sterility. Simon suddenly and passionately cried out.

'What's it all for, Hugo? What's it all about? What are we doing here making vast wads of moolah so that even more people can live in even greater social isolation in increasingly barren environments? Are we not merely prawns in an unprotected loan-infested wilderness?'

He began reciting, standing in the centre of the office, one arm outstretched theatrically.

> *'Happy are the men who yet before they are killed*
> *Can let their veins run cold*
> *Whom no compassion fleers*

*Or makes their feet
Sore on the alleys cobbled with their brothers*

'Do we care anymore, Hugo? Do we feel? Do we have compassion? And if we do, do we care enough, and about the things that really matter? Ah, Hugo! Behold this sterility and weep! Where now the alleyways of London town? Where now those hidden, winding, myriad places, replete with teeming life, endless variety and dirt.'

'Do you often quote poetry, Simon? I only ask rhetorically, as from hard experience I know only too well that you do.'

'I'm so pleased you enjoy it! And yes I quote as often as the pursuit of wealth and exploitation of the poor permit.'

He took a sheet of paper from Hugo's desk and began to fold it into a paper aeroplane.

'Be careful with those documents, Simon, and kindly don't crease that piece of paper. It's part of a very important contract. It's the culmination of that project I've been working on with Laraine.'

'Ah. The wondrous Laraine!'

Laraine was indeed wondrous - tall and spectacular, like some elegant skyscraper from her native New York. Except, unlike them, she had high, pronounced and well-rouged cheekbones. She'd come over from the New York office on temporary assignment, working tirelessly and selflessly to further both her professional and personal aspirations.

Simon launched the paper dart, which flew gracefully to the window, bent its nose and dropped to the floor. He retrieved it, smoothed it out, and replaced it on Hugo's desk.

'There you are, Hugo, and no harm done. By the way, there's something I've always been meaning to ask you. Apart from brief excursions with spectacular American stockbrokers, what on earth do you do here all day, stuck on your side of this horrible office? I've never liked it - in fact I've always felt it was the very model of sterility.'

'The sterility of an environment is very often in inverse proportion to the wealth of ideas it generates.'

'That's palpable nonsense and yet contains much that is undeniably true. But really, Hugo, what do you do here?'

'Very much the same as you do in your half of this sterile office, I assume.'

'As you must have noticed by now, I do absolutely nothing at all. And in that sense I do at least achieve a certain consonance with the sterility of the environment, if nothing else.'

'For goodness sake! All you ever talk about is sterility. Anyone would think you ran a fertility clinic.'

'Well you raised the subject, with all that risqué talk of eventualities. Talking of which, how is Pippa? I haven't seen her in ages.'

Hugo put down his pen, and turned his pensive but still highly impressive profile towards the window. That morning he'd been unable to locate his mobile, despite a frantic and extensive search. His concern was not simply due to the inconvenience and loss of contact information. What was more worrying was that for several weeks he'd been receiving explicit, anonymous texts from a stalker. At least, he assumed it was a stalker - a friend would surely not send the kind of messages he'd been getting, which were of a rather too explicitly friendly nature. And a friend would also surely not text from a hidden number. Of course he'd thought of blocking it, but wanted first to discover the identity of his correspondent. Presumably female. Hopefully so - the alternative was even more unpleasant to contemplate. And then of course the biggest worry of all - what if Pippa were to come across his mobile and look at the messages? Hugo expelled the breath he'd been unconsciously holding and looked back at

Simon, who was watching him closely and sympathetically. He cleared his throat.

'Things aren't going too well, as a matter of fact. I…I feel she's lost interest in me.'

'Surely not! Who on earth in their right mind could lose interest in you, of all people.'

'I know it sounds incredible. But this is a woman we're talking about.'

'I'd forgotten that. Carry on.'

'Well, we never seem able to show any real emotional warmth towards each other anymore. Our conversations are like some elaborate ritual with unspoken but clearly defined limits and parameters. There's never any emotional depth to any of our interactions.'

'Unlike our conversations, you mean.'

'Exactly. And because of this I've begun to wonder…'

The magnificently defined features drooped a little.

'Go on.'

'It's ridiculous, I know. My evidence is entirely circumstantial.'

'But you think…'

'I think…that is, I wonder, whether Pippa might be having an affair.'

There was a slight pause, in which the words languished and expired in the dry and airless atmosphere.

'Hugo, would you allow me to make two observations?'

'Certainly, if you think that in the absence of both evidence and rational foundation, mere observation can do any more than add layers of ambiguity to what is already opaque.'

'Never mind that - and what are you doing?'

Hugo was feeling in the pockets of the jacket hung on the back of his chair, then half rising and slipping his hands into his trouser pockets.

'Nothing - in fact very little at all,' he said, sitting down again with an abstracted air.

'Well, stop fidgeting for a moment and listen to what I have to say. Now, firstly, knowing Pippa as I do, I would trust her above and beyond anyone else that I have ever met, including even you. No offence intended, Hugo.'

'None taken. I completely agree with you. In fact - '

'As I was saying, I believe she is the sanest and finest of women.'

'I agree with you. In fact - '

'Secondly, as you must have noticed by now, all women are completely mad. Now, you may think that this second statement is at variance with the first. And it is true that in all normal circumstances Pippa would appear as sane as you or I. But - she is still a woman.'

'If you would permit me to speak, I would say that in fact that's exactly the problem. And it's one that appears to defy solution.'

'I'm not so sure. Let's try to look at this objectively. Let's try to understand the dynamics of the problem from their perspective. For the sake of argument, say you take what a woman says, reverse it, divide by 5.3 and then subtract any number that comes into your head. Now what are you left with?'

'I've no idea.'

'Neither have I. But that was just a random example. What I'm trying to say is that with sufficient mental contortions, sustained for a possibly indefinite period, a woman's brain might eventually, possibly, arrive at something approximating to the truth. I say might. Where women are involved there is no certainty. In the minds of women the laws of logic fluctuate like tendrils of lost dreams strewn hither and yon by careless zephyrs. Truth, to women, is no more than yesterday's discarded desires. It is an infinitely flexible instrument, wonderfully adaptable to all situations and circumstances.'

'I would like to say, Simon, that you are being very unfair.'

'I'm sure you would, Hugo. So would all who live to see such times. But it is not given to us at this moment to dispute hard facts.'

'You speak of women in the collective as if they were so many potatoes or consignments of machine tools. Surely you allow for some variation as regards character and intellect?'

'Certainly I have noticed a wide variation in outward appearance.'

'Close enough.'

'What I'm trying to say is, that if you're expecting a logical explanation for Pippa's behaviour, you're wasting your time. Instead you must look for some instinctive, emotional motive behind her actions. Look, why don't you invite me for dinner? I can observe the situation first-hand, talk or rather listen diplomatically to Pippa, and hopefully allay your fears.'

'Okay. How about tomorrow?'

'Fine.'

'Fine. I'll just give Pippa a quick ring.'

Hugo began opening the drawers of his desk, rifling noisily through the contents.

'You appear once more to be at something of a loss, Hugo.'

'It's my mobile. It's disappeared.'

'Try that instead,' said Simon, pointing to the telephone on the desk. Hugo looked at it for several moments, as if remembering something buried deep in his subconscious. Then picked up the receiver and dialled.

3

Pippa at her desk. A tall brunette, with centrally parted hair cut to a stylish medium length. Her high forehead, intelligent dark brown eyes and long, aerodynamic nose were of a pattern derived from her father, a retired civil servant.

At last she'd found the courage to bring Hugo's mobile out from her bag, and was now gently handling it, wearing a frown and perplexed expression. She ran her fingers over its buttons, trying to will herself to switch it on. Then sighed, put it on the desk directly in front of her, and began to think instead, with delicious, hungry, revengeful desire, of going straight out and buying those adorable pink Armani jeans she'd had her eye on for ages! Or that fab little bracelet from Karen Millen! Or that yummy Prada handbag - God, she'd wanted that from the first moment she'd seen it. Or maybe just those amazing shiny high-heeled boots from Ralph Lauren! Oh, they're so fab! Or maybe she would just buy them all! Every last one of them! And to hell with him! And to hell with their bloody credit card! Anyway, she'd just hide the bill from him. No, she wouldn't - she'd present it to him! She'd hold it out towards him, she'd brandish it at him with her chin tilted high in the air, she'd shake it in his face. There, Hugo! There! Now see what you've made me do, you...you cheating little...snake! It's all your doing, with your secrecy, your possible infidelity, your strange silences and your - for God's sake, pull yourself together woman! You have no evidence at all. It's all circumstantial and instinctive, nothing more than feminine intuition. Oh God! Oh God! I just can't look at it!

She jumped as the phone on her desk rang, and scrabbled to pick up the receiver.

'Hello?'

'Hello, darling. It's me - Hugo.'

'Oh hello, darling. I...I was just thinking about you.'

'Were you, darling?'

'Yes, of course darling. I'm always thinking about you, darling, nearly.'

'Are you, darling? How nice of you to be always thinking about me, nearly. Are you even nearly thinking about me when you're thinking about something entirely different, darling?'

'Yes darling, especially then. Anyway, to what do I owe the pleasure of this call?'

'Well, I was wondering if I could invite someone to dinner tomorrow night.'

'Were you? And…did you have anyone specific in mind?'

'Yes, of course. I would hardly invite some random person off the street.'

'No, no, of course not, darling. Who, then, is the lucky invitee?'

'Is that a real word, darling?'

'Do I question your knowledge of shares, bonds, mutual funds, hedge funds, derivatives or operational risks?'

'I'm sorry. I didn't mean to question your expert knowledge, although of course the English language is our common heritage and therefore not strictly speaking an area of exclusive speciality. Anyway, the invitee is Simon, of course.'

'Why of course? I'm sure you have a great many friends.'

'Yes, I'm sure I do, darling. But in this particular instance it is, in fact, Simon. He suggested that I invite him for dinner.'

'Did he? How very accommodating of him.'

'You don't mind, do you?'

'Of course not. Why should I mind? In fact, now that you mention it, an idea occurs to me.'

'Does it, darling? How wonderfully creative of you!'

'The thing is we're having a few little problems here at the office. Policy issues, really, but you know how quickly such things can descend into personality conflicts, especially when people don't express their true feelings or tell the truth about things. I'm coming to believe that's the most important thing anyone can ever do. And at least you can't say that about Sally.'

'I wouldn't dream of saying anything of the kind about Sally. But where exactly is all this leading?'

'Sally, as you know,' continued Pippa, ignoring Hugo's interjection, 'perhaps sometimes goes a little too far the other way. She has such strong opinions that she can ruffle anybody's feathers, and Araminta's in particular. So why don't we make it a dinner party, and invite Sally and Araminta. Perhaps being away from the working environment will give them an opportunity to build some bridges.'

'And perhaps even bring calm to their troubled waters.'

'I knew you'd understand, darling.'

Picking up the mobile once again, she began handling it with nervous delicacy. Feeling as if her entire future, in all its intimate detail, might be laid bare within its plastic casing.

'By the way, darling, I'm sure you'd have told me already if you had, but I don't suppose you've seen my mobile anywhere, have you?'

Pippa jumped with a half-stifled cry. The mobile escaped her grasp and fell with a clatter onto the desk.

'Hello, darling? Are you still there? What was that noise?'

'I...I...it was the stapler. I dropped the stapler. I was holding it and then quite suddenly - without warning, in fact - it seemed to literally jump out of my hand. I don't know what happened, but it was just the stapler. And...um...it doesn't seem to be damaged at all...thank goodness...but then, it doesn't really matter, does it. It's only a stapler, after all, and they're really quite sturdy - they're not the kind of thing that's likely to break if you...I hope not, anyway...it was just the stapler.'

In the silence that followed she looked down at the mobile, willing it not to have been damaged and that her future, with or without intimate detail, might remain forever obscure. Hugo's voice, sounding suddenly grave and serious, made her jump once more.

'So you dropped the stapler. I'm pleased and relieved that it appears undamaged. But to return to my question, I don't suppose you've come across my mobile?'

'No darling, no - no I haven't - I haven't seen your...'

There was a knock at the door.

'Have to go, darling - there's someone at the door - sorry, darling - it was the stapler. Bye, darling.'

She slammed down the phone as the door opened, and into the room came Araminta, and the room suddenly filled with the promise of spring and secret trysts in hidden, leafy arbours and the scent of desperate longing and of poignant, lost romance.

At twenty seven, Araminta was a little younger than Pippa, a little older than Sally, and decidedly less amiable than either. Highly feminine to all outward appearances - a femininity strangely at odds with her specialist genre of faux-realism and explicit violence - she displayed a kind of neutral, almost inoffensive attractiveness, the kind of broad-beamed prettiness which declines swiftly into dumpy anonymity past the forty mark. A querulous manner, equally demanding of attention and approval, seemed perversely calculated to annoy Sally, but conversely produced a protective compassion in Freddy. And though her specialisation in thrillers and sex crimes could have been the result of conscious choice, in fact she'd quickly understood soon after joining the firm where Freddy's tastes lay. And soon after that discovered her own tastes lay in a similar direction and along similar lines, so that it was not long before submissions of that type were steered her way.

Pippa snatched the mobile from her desk top and threw it into her handbag by the chair. She closed her eyes for a moment, rubbed her forehead, then sat back in her chair and looked up at Araminta with what she hoped was a welcoming smile.

'Sit down, Araminta. Let's have a little chat.'

She waved a hand at the chair in front of her desk, and waited while Araminta settled herself. Thinking as Araminta flicked her long hair behind her shoulders that if she only smiled a little more she would actually be quite agreeably pretty.

'Darling, I'd just like to have a quick word about your working relationship with Sally.'

Araminta's face took on a grim cast, slightly compromising her feminine allure.

'Of course, it's to be expected that people will have differences of opinion from time to time, and it's good that we can express those differences. But with you and Sally, it so often seems to descend quickly into acrimony.'

'Well it's her! She's always so rude! And she's always making fun of somebody, or pulling what we do to pieces. She obviously doesn't like her job - or books - so I don't know why she does it at all.'

'Darling, I know she has very strong opinions, and she often doesn't express them with any great tact.'

'That's quite a concession from you, Pippa!'

'But I don't think she does it gratuitously, just to offend people.'

'Don't you? Didn't you hear some of her comments at the meeting today? Some of the things she said were just horrible, personal comments. And not just directed at me, though often they are. I just don't think she should be allowed to do it and get away with it all the time.'

'It's not a question of getting away with it, darling.'

'Yes, it is - when does anybody ever pull her into line, or dare question anything she says?'

'Darling, I specifically told her to apologise to you, which she then did.'

'You call that an apology? Her so-called apology was more insulting than anything she'd said previously. Especially to Freddy. In fact, within the space of a few minutes she'd managed to insult me, Jemima and Freddy, as well as declaring most of what we produce here as worthless rubbish. I just find it so negative and demotivating.'

'Look, I do take your point and I will have a word with Sally. But please bear in mind that to have a strong, independent voice within the firm is a real asset. She often provides a different perspective to the other members of the editorial team, and it is important that she has the courage to voice her opinions. I know it's not always a comfortable process, and that sometimes egos can be a little bruised - I've been on the receiving end myself a few times - but I think - '

'I knew you'd take her side!'

'Darling, I'm not taking her side. I will speak to her, and ask her to moderate her personal comments.'

'And it's always other people's egos getting bruised! Why not ever hers?'

'Look, darling, Hugo and I are throwing a little dinner party tomorrow night, and we'd really like you to come.'

'Is Sally coming?'

'I...don't know yet, darling. I haven't asked her. Possibly.'

'Well, I can't come then.'

'Araminta, you and Sally have to learn to work together. You have to find a way of getting on together. And that's why I want the two of you to meet in a nice, relaxed environment, away from all the pressures of work, but with other people around so that you don't end up hurting each other. I'm sure you'll get along splendidly! And you'll probably find you've got lots in common.'

'I doubt that.'

'Will you come, darling? Please? We're also inviting Hugo's friend, Simon - oh, and Freddy, although I haven't actually asked him yet.'

Araminta's expression cleared.

'Oh, alright. But I'm only coming because you've asked me - I wouldn't come for anybody else.'

'I appreciate that, darling. Although it would be difficult for the invitation to legitimately come from anybody else. Anyway, we'll look forward to you coming enormously, darling. Now, I don't suppose you could just call into Sally's office and ask her to pop in to see me, could you?'

Alone once more, Pippa looked blankly across at the large, artistic, framed photograph of the London Eye reflected in the Thames, perpetually in her eyeline. Then she reached down and again drew the mobile from her handbag. She closed her eyes, drew a deep breath and steeled herself. Then with a slight pressing movement, and a tiny click, she turned on the mobile. There were two new text messages. With all her being focused on the screen, she clicked once more, then waited a moment for the first message to appear.

4

She felt small, incalculably stupid. As if, in fact, the most stupid and undesirable creature that had ever existed. She could understand perfectly why Hugo thought her so unbearably mundane. Forced to find consolation in the arms of some exotic, sensual love bunny. Some creature with the longest legs, slimmest waist, most mesmerising eyes, most golden blonde hair and highest IQ of anything that had ever existed. How stupid. Unbearably stupid.

With trembling fingers she slowly pushed the mobile to one side of her desk, then laid down her head and sobbed. She wanted to scream but had neither the energy nor will. Only oblivion would serve now. The total absence of feeling.

She felt a hand on her head, and looked up into Sally's warm eyes looking compassionately into hers. Without words Pippa half rose, Sally's arm around her shoulders as she collapsed against her, weeping without restraint. Sally cradled her head, stroking her face, running her fingers through Pippa's hair, murmuring incoherent consolations.

It was some time before she seemed calmer. Sally drew a chair alongside, then put her arm once more around Pippa's shoulders.

'Pippa, what is it? What's wrong?'

Pippa wiped her eyes with a tissue, blew her nose, glanced at Sally - a desolate look - then stared at her desk top. The neat piles of manuscripts, the telephone, the stapler. Hugo's mobile.

'I don't think he loves me anymore.'

'Who - Hugo?'

'Yes, of course - Hugo, my husband.'

'Why do you say that?'

There was a long silence.

'I...we haven't been communicating properly for a while. It's as if we've run out of things to say to each other.'

'Ah. I wonder if there's a formula for calculating precisely the instant when married couples discover they've run out of things to say to each other. That heart-rending moment when physical attraction is abruptly compromised by the words coming from the beloved's mouth - mere counterfeits of what was once fresh, exciting and original.'

'You talk as if you've been married yourself. Anyway, we hadn't run out of things to say to each other - I mean, we hadn't before…'

'Before you did?'

'No, I don't mean that. I mean that something changed a few weeks ago. Hugo changed. He became…not quite himself. Somehow distant, preoccupied.'

'Not quite his normal ebullient self? Well, it happens now and then to all of us. Problems at work, Third World debt, car troubles, finding a clean pair of socks. It could be anything. Look, Hugo might have his faults, but - '

'What faults?' said Pippa, looking up suddenly.

'Well, he's impossibly handsome for a start. I've never seen so many features so perfectly arranged. The man's a standing public attraction, not to mention private allurement, and that sort of thing should surely be licensed, if not actively discouraged.'

Pippa's expression became suddenly dreamy.

'Do you really think he's so very handsome?'

'Oh come on, Pippa. We can hardly overstate our case here, can we. His eyes are like high interest deposit bonds, his lips a perfectly executed merger, his skin the translucent clarity of an investment portfolio, and as for the tilt and angle of that chin - '

'Sally, don't be silly,' said Pippa with a small smile.

'Pippa, he's gorgeous. If he was any more gorgeous you'd need a lethal weapon certificate.

And he loves you, and only you - I'm sure of it. Most men might be about as reliable as a Skoda in a sandstorm - forgive the lapse from my humanist convictions - but Hugo is one of those rare men that I would put complete faith in. I would vouch for his integrity. Of course, some might say he's a little wooden and predictable - not me, I hasten to add,' responding quickly to Pippa's look. 'But I'm absolutely certain that you have nothing to worry about. Look, if you're not communicating properly, then do something about it. Express yourself! Express your emotions! That's what they're there for! They're not there just to inconvenience us and disturb the smooth trajectory of our lives. They're what we are and the reason we exist. So don't be afraid - go ahead and express them! Openly and fully! Now! Today!'

'You don't understand. It's not just about lack of communication. There's something else.'

'What else?'

She cast a tear-stained glance at Sally. Then pointed at Hugo's mobile lying on her desk.

'That.'

'It's a mobile. So what?'

Pippa reached out slowly, as if fearing the mobile would scald her hand. In silence she clicked on menu, messages, inbox.

'It's not my mobile, it's Hugo's.'

'Well, this might seem like a very obvious question, but why have you got Hugo's mobile?'

'I told you, things haven't been right between us for some time.'

'Right. So you pinched his mobile to see what little secrets you could find out?'

'Yes. I mean no, of course I didn't pinch it. I just…borrowed it for the day.'

'Without telling Hugo, I suppose?'

Pippa nodded.

'And now he's wondering where it is?'

'Yes.'

'Okay, so what's the payoff? You've obviously found something out, and presumably not something you wanted to.'

Without a word Pippa handed the mobile to Sally. For several minutes and in complete silence Sally examined the texts in question. Then she sat back, and placed the mobile on the desk.

'These don't prove anything. Were there any messages in the sent box?'

'No, I checked that. But then he'd hardly leave incriminating messages in there, would he?'

'No more than he would leave incriminating received texts, if he had any reason to feel guilt at receiving them.'

'Perhaps they have some sentimental value to him.'

Her voice tainted with unaccustomed bitterness.

'Pippa, I agree that on the face of it this doesn't look good. But this is one of those strange, confusing but critical moments in your life when you must look beyond this slim evidence and simply have faith in Hugo. Is there anything beyond these imaginative texts to lead you in any way to question his probity?'

'No.'

'Very well. Then now is the moment to say, I believe in Hugo, I know he is loyal to me, therefore there must be an alternative, if not necessarily rational, explanation for him having received these messages. And what method should you employ to discover that explanation?'

Pippa shook her head.

'I don't know.'

'It's quite simple. You ask Hugo.'

A look of horror spread over Pippa's face.

'I can't. I simply can't. He'd know I'd looked at his private text messages.'

Sally's face mingled scorn and amazement.

'Private text messages? You married people are seriously weird! You'll be telling me next you have separate bank accounts.'

Pippa looked at her with a half-smile.

'You have, haven't you! My God, what a strange conception of loyalty and togetherness you people have. Do you actually sleep in the same bed, or is that something negotiated by your lawyers?'

'Sally, please.'

'Okay, okay. Now look, having a passion for something or somebody, having emotions - it means taking a risk. It means exposing yourself to the possibility of ridicule. It means risking being wrong, and therefore being humbled or hurt in some way. But that's what you have to do, Pippa. You have to risk being wrong about Hugo. You have to put your body and soul, your whole faith and your belief in him on the line. Yes, that carries the risk that you will be proved wrong, and that he is cheating on you. And if you have exposed yourself by going out on a limb with your emotions, it will hurt all the more if he has betrayed you. But being alive entails taking a risk for what you truly believe in. And that includes being hurt by betrayal. But once we stop doing that, once we stop reaching out and exposing ourselves emotionally, we might just as well be dead.'

Pippa cast a hopeful, childlike look at Sally.

'What should I do?'

'Tonight, when you're alone together, just behave in a normal, friendly way as if you hadn't a care in the world. Don't put him on the defensive. Just mention casually that you found his phone, noticed that there were a couple of received texts on it, and thought they must be from you. And so you read them, with the others. Make a joke out of it. Make him believe you have a sense of humour. Smile a lot - giggle, even, if you must. Say, These are funny texts, Hugo! Is it - who's that guy he shares an office with?'

'Simon.'

'Is it Simon playing a joke on you? Do you get what I'm driving at, Pippa? Give him the room and space to relax, so that he can tell you the truth about those texts. It's far more likely that he will if you treat it in a light-hearted way, rather than push him into a corner and make him all defensive.'

'Okay. I'm sure you're right, Sally. I'll try to do it tonight.'

'Don't try. Do it. Look, I really like the guy. He has so little ego, especially considering his extraordinary physical assets. I'm sure if Hugo met himself in a narrow lane, he would courteously step aside. And that's what I like most about him. He's civilized, unlike so many people. So I really think you're wrong to doubt him, Pippa. Just have faith.'

'Darling, I don't know how to thank you. I feel better already. Your words have given me new strength and hope. Will you come to dinner tomorrow night?'

Sally laughed.

'You don't have to feed me in return for my great wisdom, Pippa. My advice comes free of charge. And incidentally, it's your responsibility if you act upon it.'

Pippa smiled, looking almost cheerful.

'You are a silly! And yes, I understand it's my responsibility, of course. But in fact I wanted to have a little dinner party with a few people from here, and - '

'Who?'

'Well, I thought perhaps you…'

'Yes.'

'And me, of course…'

'Yes.'

'And possibly Freddy…'

'Yes.'

'Although I haven't asked him yet.'

'And…'

'And…possibly…well, I was thinking, maybe… Araminta.'

'Dear old Minty! Don't you think it's bad enough having to spend time with her here, without seeking the dear old thing out to enjoy her social charms.'

'You know, Sally, I really want you and Araminta to get to know each other better. She really likes you, I'm sure.'

'You know very well that neither of us likes the other at all. And a better acquaintance would surely only lead to the flourishing of an even warmer mutual antipathy.'

'I'm sure that need not be the case. Now - can I assume that you're free tomorrow night?'

'Not necessarily. I may be required by unforeseen circumstances to invent some long-standing sudden occurrence that will prevent me from attending.'

'Oh Sally - do come! I need your support. Your proximity will give me superadded confidence.'

'I think you underestimate my superfluous attractions.'

'And you could tell me how you think Hugo is behaving.'

'I'm sure he'll behave with all that lack of style and charisma for which he is renowned. The dullness of his personality will be undermined only by his paucity of wit.'

'Is that a yes, then, Sally?'

'Oh God, if you insist!'

5

Hugo's Porsche crept cautiously alongside Pippa's Golf. Crouching like some wild beast at bay. Hugo listening with consoling but only momentary satisfaction to the deep throb of the horizontally-opposed, air-cooled six. Pausing in the sudden, thick silence.

By the illumination of the interior light he carefully examined the bedroom eyes and chiselled features. He moved his head this way and that. And yet, with all his striving for objectivity, it was impossible withal to detect diminution of effect or evidence of declining powers. No - even after the most thorough inspection he was forced to believe that whatever was amiss had its roots elsewhere. And certainly not in the aesthetics department.

Pippa looked up as Hugo entered the bright, spacious kitchen. Her eyes searched his unsmiling features, smiling herself in anxious and contrived affect. Turning back, immersing herself in preparations. Striving consciously to keep Sally's words at the forefront of her mind - the need to achieve a front of normality. When she spoke, her voice seemed only slightly higher than usual.

'How has your day been, darling?'

'I've had a not entirely unpleasant day, darling. Although a fairly entirely unpleasant one.'

'That's lovely, darling!'

'Yes, in fact I find my resistance to unpleasantness waning almost by the second, to the point of being hardly able to distinguish it from any other negative/repellent emotion.'

'That's wonderful, darling. I'm so pleased.'

'Darling?'

'Yes, darling?'

'Do you ever listen to a word I say?'

'That's lovely, d - I mean...darling, I don't suppose you could get me a dry martini, could you?'

Hugo moved swiftly to the drinks cabinet.

'I said I intend driving for Ferrari next year. Here you are, darling.'

'Do you, dear? That's lovely, darling. Thank you. Mmm, that's wonderful.' Oh my God, he's so stern and serious! Why? Why? Keep talking! 'Now, darling, I wonder if I should put these in now, or if I should leave them for tomorrow, but I thought if I do as much as possible tonight, there'll be less to do tomorrow.'

'Your logic is unassailable.'

'I know, darling. But you know, in many ways I wish I'd got somebody in to do the catering, but then that would be a complete waste of money, not that money matters so very much in the grand scheme of things.'

'Darling, do you think meaningful communication between two people is a necessary adjunct to cohabitation?'

Pippa set down her glass with trembling fingers.

'Er…what do you mean, my sweetheart?'

'Although I suppose I may decide on John Player Team Lotus in the end.'

'I don't suppose you could help me to…'

'Yes, of course, my love. How small would you like the pieces?'

'I do so hope Sally likes Simon. I think he could be just her type. That's fine, darling.'

'And of course the statement was intentionally paradoxical.'

'That's lovely, Hugo. Thanks, darling.'

'Darling?'

'Yes, darling?'

'You seem to be speaking a little strangely, darling.'

'Do I darling? In what way, pray?'

'Well, in the sort of way that nobody in real life ever speaks. In fact, in a sort of affected and entirely insincere style which nobody outside a very poor pulp romantic novel would ever dare to speak for fear of immediate and justified reprisal.'

'Oh!' exclaimed Pippa. 'My dearest one, please forgive me! My head is so full of romcom. And also, very often lately, of chick lit, not to mention...well, nothing else, really, of course. Nothing at all.'

'My love, do not they often overlap?'

'Oh they do, my sweet, they do - more often than one would think or wish. And in fact I'm not sure how many more romcom or chick lit novels I can possibly read, or have sufficient faith in to actually commission, or suggest pink and green flowery covers for, without being violently ill in one form or another.'

'Isn't that just the kind of thing Sally comes out with? I'm sure I've heard you comment about her outbursts in the past.'

How does he know I've been speaking to Sally? How on earth does he - oh yes, we work at the same place! I remember! Keep focusing, for God's sake. Get a grip!

'Yes, you're quite right, darling, and the trouble is, I think I'm beginning to agree with her. But what Sally can't see is that publishing is a business, not some philanthropic activity or artistic indulgence. Her head is permanently in the clouds, wrapped up in some romantic vision of pure literature. But at the end of the day the books have to be balanced - I mean the books of accounts -

and profits have to be made if we're to stay in business. So we have to sell the stuff that people want to buy. That's it, I'm afraid - end of story. And in the final analysis it's my neck on the chopping block if we don't publish what we know will sell. You know, I sometimes think, Hugo, that my job is even less creative than yours.'

'My dearest darling!' said Hugo, suddenly moving beside her and wrapping her tentatively in his arms. 'You know, you somehow always manage to say the right thing!'

Oh my God! I can't cope with physical contact - not at this moment.

'Thank you, darling. But do mind the knife, darling, as it's extremely sharp.'

Hugo carefully detached himself, and cast a speculative look at the knife in Pippa's right hand. She was trembling at the sudden closeness, part of her desperate to throw herself once more into his arms.

'But, as you know, Sally is so uncompromising. And yes, of course I admire her for having the courage of her convictions. But real life is, as we both know, a series of compromises.'

Hugo looked closely at Pippa's face for any indication of layers of encapsulated meaning. But her expression, like any potential layers of meaning, remained encapsulated.

'That's a good point. By the way - and to change the subject slightly - can I ask what you're making for tomorrow, darling?'

'Of course, sweet one. We're having a variety of these little - well, I don't know quite how to - and then perhaps a sauce of - well, I haven't decided exactly yet what kind of - and then I thought if I served them with perhaps just a little - well, I'll just have to see what seems appropriate nearer to the - and then for dessert perhaps just a sprinkling of - well, I'm not exactly sure of their - over the top of a variety of - well, I'll see what looks freshest and most - oh, and coffee to finish, that's what I was trying to remember - and then perhaps - '

'That all sounds absolutely wonderful. And sorry to interrupt your frank enunciation of that delicious menu, but I was just wondering if you'd happened to come across my mobile since you got back?'

The sharp knife flew out of Pippa's hand, and she spun round, her face pale, pink, crimson and white in quick succession.

'No, no I haven't - yes, yes it's here, darling, it's just over here, I found it for you - I mean I found it by chance. It was underneath something, or by the side of something, or on top of something, I can't remember which, but anyway it doesn't matter, I found it darling, and I put it here, just for you. And I...I left it switched off.'

With shaking hands she passed the mobile to Hugo. He took it and looked at it, his honed features impenetrably grave, his expression unreadable.

'Thank you, Pippa. Where did you say you'd found it?'

'I…I…I can't…it was…does it really matter, darling?'

'No, of course it doesn't really matter, darling. I'm just pleased to have it back. You say it was switched off?'

Oh my God! I've said the wrong thing again!

'I…yes, I think so, darling. I'm fairly certain that it - '

'That's strange, as I'm sure I switched it on this morning.'

'Well, that is quite strange, darling. Perhaps… perhaps it switched itself off in the course of the day.'

'That's certainly possible, although it's not really of a type that does switch itself off in the course of the day. Unless the battery is low, which in this particular instance was clearly not the case.'

'Perhaps it recharged itself somehow, and then switched itself off.'

She looked hopefully at the mobile, as if willing it to audibly concur. Though she quickly realised that it would perhaps not be able to remember in any great detail due to being switched off. Hugo looked at her with an indecipherable expression.

'I think that's somehow unlikely. If it had been switched on, do you think you would have noticed if there had been any messages on it?'

Pippa's expression changed abruptly.

'That's an astonishingly hypothetical question, and one that I must, therefore, disdain to answer.' Hugo looked mildly astonished. 'If you are able to accept my word that the phone was, indeed, switched off when I gave it to you,' continued Pippa, 'then surely the question as to whether there were any messages on it must remain quite entirely irrelevant.'

'Yes, I take your point, but - '

'And I am quite entirely uninterested in any of the messages on your mobile that you may or may not have received. Why, indeed, should I be interested in them?'

'I didn't really say you were interested in them, my darling. I was just asking whether - '

'I don't make a habit of reading other people's text messages.'

'I'm sure you don't, darling. I - '

'Only if I had a particular reason for doing so would I dream of reading someone else's text messages.'

'I'm sure of that, darling. I - '

'And I'm sure that's not the case in this instance, is it?'

'What - '

'That I had a particular reason for doing so.'

'Reason - '

'For reading the messages.'

'No, of course not, darling. And in any case, in this particular instance, as you've said yourself, the phone was switched off. So how could you have read any messages? Even if there were any, which you've said there weren't, and which of course you wouldn't have read if there were.'

'No, I didn't say there weren't any. I said that it was impossible if not unlikely that I would know, due to the mobile being switched off, and yes of course I wouldn't have read them if it hadn't been.'

Hugo appeared lost in thought, or possibly confusion.

'I'm staying at home tomorrow, by the way,' said Pippa.

'Are you, darling? Why are you - '

'You'll be going to work tomorrow as normal, I take it?'

'Yes, darling, I - '

'Good. I will spend tomorrow preparing for our party. Now, I have a headache and I'm going upstairs.'

Pippa swept from the room and slammed the door. There was a degree of aesthetic disturbance to Hugo's features - an unfortunate side effect of the perplexing turn of events.

6

Sally possessed a gravitational pull out of all proportion to her size. Like a small, compact star, she created a sizeable impression on the fabric of space around her, pulling disparate persons and personalities into her orbit. One of which was Daniel. To what extent his siding with her in literary matters was due to the unusual violet definition of her eyes would be difficult to say. But so often did he drop in to her office, and also explicitly agree with her in staff meetings, that Sally had begun to suspect that he must be by now, as was often the case, desperately in love with her.

In a spirit of compassion and generosity, she therefore decided to deflect him towards the more modest but realistic orbit of Jemima, who anyway, through observation of her behaviour, Sally knew to be particularly keen on Daniel.

'Oh God, I seem to have done it again!' said Daniel, as Jemima once more fled the room in tears. 'I never mean to upset her, but it seems that every time I open my mouth she has an emotional breakdown.'

'Are you blind? Do you really not know what's going on?'

He shook his head.

'She's in love. With you.'

'What?'

'Yes. Head over heels in love. Lucky boy! She's quite a catch!'

'I can't believe it. You really think so?'

'Too good to believe, eh? Yes, I'm sure of it. And you really ought to go after her, you know. I'm sure she's fully expecting it by now.'

'But I've never thought of her in that way. Or in any way in particular.'

'And now the blinding light of revelation. Well, go ahead and ask her out. You've got so much in common - both of you in publishing, both getting on a bit. You don't want to leave it too late and miss the boat completely.'

'I do kind of like her.'

'Well, there you are then. That's settled. Now go after her, Daniel.'

She took up the pen she'd laid down.

'I'll go and find her in a minute. There was something else, Sally.'

'What?'

'Something I wanted to ask you. Your opinion about something.'

'You couldn't have done better. It's well known that I have opinions to spare, though rarely are they agreed with, and more rarely still acted upon.'

'That's what I thought. I mean that I couldn't have done better.'

'Well, what is it?'

'The thing is, I've been doing a bit of writing.'

Sally sighed.

'Daniel, I never recommend writing to anyone working in publishing. It always results in such an inferiority complex that any old piece of drivel that comes through the door is automatically regarded as a masterpiece. No wonder tripe gets such an easy ride in places like this. Give it up, before your judgement is permanently impaired.'

His eyes looked pained behind the heavy frames.

'I was joking. What exactly have you been writing, Daniel?'

He immediately moved to the edge of his chair, and his hands became animated.

'Well, I've been working on this sci-fi novel. What happens is this guy takes over an entire universe, somehow takes control of it - I haven't worked out all the details yet - but then in reaction to his repressive rule a few people - aliens, of course - start this completely passive resistance movement which inadvertently results in a catastrophic failure of the whole fabric of interplanetary society. And...well, that's just a brief overview, of course. So what do you think of it - conceptually, I mean?'

Sally opened her eyes, and took a deep breath.

'Daniel, I'm afraid I'm not really into science fiction.'

'This isn't science fiction as such - well, it is, but that's really just the frame. What matters is how the characters relate to each other - their emotions, the paradox inherent in their struggle for a free universe from the shackles of inaction and so on.'

'Right. Well, it certainly sounds interesting, and - I tell you what, you work on it, and then when you've got it more fully developed come back to me and I'll have a look at it. How about that?'

'That's wonderful, Sally! Thank you. To have my work read - by you in particular - '

At this moment the door slowly opened and Jemima crept back into the room, eyes down, a tissue to her nose. Daniel watched as if seeing her for the first time.

'Jemima, I'm...Sally and I were just...are you okay?'

'Hello, Daniel,' she sniffed. 'I'm sorry, I had something in my eye.'

'I'm very sorry. Is it out now?'

'What?'

'The thing that was in your eye.'

'Oh, yes. Completely. Thanks.'
'I'm very pleased.'
A long silence.
'Well, I suppose I must be going.'
He walked slowly to the door, paused, looking back at Jemima.
'I hope we'll...I hope to see you again soon, Jemima.'
Jemima's eyes flickered towards Daniel. She uttered something inaudible and sniffed.

After Daniel had left, Jemima glanced timidly a number of times towards Sally, punctuated by the occasional sniffle. Receiving no acknowledgement, she at last coughed and cleared her throat.
'Sally,' said Jemima hesitantly. 'What do you think of Daniel?'
'I never think of him, if I can help it.'
'But you were talking to him just now.'
'I especially never think of him when I'm talking to him. I find to do so upsets my parameters of good taste, not to mention my digestion.'
Jemima looked crestfallen.
'Oh for God's sake, Jemima, just tell him you're in love with him, and give us all a break.'
'What do you mean?'
Sally looked up once more from her manuscript at Jemima's pensive expression.

'Which part of what I said confused you?'
'Why do you say I'm in love with him?'
'Oh please! I haven't got time or inclination for a Socratic question and answer session just now.'
'Well...what should I say - what should I do?'
Sally put down her pen with a sigh.
'Well, the first thing to do if you fancy a man is to transform yourself into something that you're clearly not. Which means, in your case, and starting with your face, you need to wipe at least fifteen years off, if possible. This will involve cleansing your spots, plucking your eyebrows, dyeing your roots, plus all additional make-up and general maintenance work as necessary. Now, turning to the rest of your body. Let's see - if you mean to take your clothes off at any point you'll need to massage all that cellulite. Oh, and give some thought to those stomach muscles, which I'm afraid look pretty flabby to me. Then you'll need to wax your legs, pumice your feet, exfoliate and moisturize your skin - oh, and don't forget to shave under your arms - and anywhere else you can think of. And - well, I think that's probably about the lot. Shouldn't take more than three or four evenings.'
Jemima's face had collapsed to the floor.
'Do I really need...I haven't got...I mean, I wouldn't know how to do half those things, Sally.'

'Well, those are the rules. Don't blame me if you refuse to conform to them. Only if you do all those things, without exception, will you provoke his interest. And then he'll treat you like shit, cheat on you, and finally dump you by text. What more could a romantic heroine possibly want?'

Jemima started sniffling again.

'For Christ's sake, you should know the way it's done by now. You read that kind of stuff by the cartload. In fact that tripe we were discussing earlier, and that you were pushing, is a prime example. Too bad Daniel didn't like it.'

Jemima's snuffles became a flood of tears, and she rushed from the room. Sally's eyes widened for a moment, before shaking her head, picking up her pen, and finding her place again. After half a minute or so came a gentle knock on the door.

'For God's sake! Can't anyone ever leave me alone?'

Freddy popped his good-natured face around the door frame.

'Sally, could I have a quick word?'

'No, not at the moment. I'm busy.'

'Okay. Well, when do you think you could fit me in?'

'What is it, Freddy?'

She was frowning, her biro making occasional quick movements across the page.

'I just thought it might be useful to have a quick clear-the-air sort of chat, if you've got time.'

'Oh, I get it! Dear old Minty's been spilling the beans, has she?'

Freddy sidled apologetically into the room. Tall, sandy-haired, amiable features. Mid to late fifties. Sally's critique of his abilities was possibly unfair. It's true he did like his thrillers, crime and sex stories, and the more creative the method of killing and inflicting pain, and the deeper the level of sexual deviancy, the greater his enjoyment. But whether he derived more pleasure from this than from an aesthetic appreciation of the flow of the prose or the quality of the imagery was open to question. Certainly the extent of his predilection for the depiction of extreme violence in all its forms did seem in curiously inverse proportion to a mild and gentle nature. He must have got something right, however - the company had managed to keep its head above the predatory waters of publishing for the past thirty years or so, when many had disappeared in a blood-red frenzy of exsanguination. He glanced at the empty desk opposite Sally's.

'Where's Jemima?'

'Haven't a clue. In the toilets reconstructing her face, probably.'

Freddy perched precariously on the edge of Jemima's desk.

'Sally, do you enjoy your work here?'

She raised her head from the manuscript she'd resumed examining, and directed a searching gaze. An untidy mass of dark frizzy hair nicely framed a pair of fiercely intelligent yet warm blue eyes, now fixed unwaveringly upon his own. He shifted uncomfortably. Freddy had the gift of always being able to sense accurately when he was outgunned, but rationalised his limitations by considering that the ability to accurately gauge the limits of one's capacities was perhaps the greatest gift of all.

'Well, that raises an interesting question, Freddy.'

He smiled indulgently. He found it impossible not to like Sally. Though he could appreciate that those, like Araminta, who habitually stood in the firing line, might have a different perspective.

'What question is that, Sally?'

'Whether work that you enjoy is work.'

'I'm sure work has many meanings.'

'Oh, I'm sure it does. In fact my dictionary lists over thirty separate, though often related, definitions. But work as it is usually understood and generally employed means a duty or a task. It's what people have to get up in the morning to do five or six days a week, even if they're feeling like shit, as the only available means of paying the bills and subsisting. Not, therefore, a pleasure or a creative exercise, but just a job. The creative side we leave to those Titans of literature - those daughters of Uranus - all the Pennys, Emmas, Sophies and Harriets that nobly prop up the cultural life of our nation.'

'And is that how you see your work here, Sally - as just a job?'

'It's just a job when what I read is rubbish. Which is eighty or ninety percent of the time. But now and again you read something and you think - wow! I want this to be seen, I want this to be read - this makes me think and it moves me. It's just a pity you publish so much bilge, Freddy. You know, there are good writers out there - people with ideas, and with fresh, interesting ways of expressing those ideas. It's just a crying shame that they don't often get the chance to get into print, because we, like every other publisher, put all our effort and energy into supporting and publishing the tripe - the effluent of talentless automatons, linguistic timeservers and emotional derelicts.'

'I think you're being a little unfair. We do take a chance, sometimes, and publish original, creative and innovative works. But they're never going to be big sellers, Sally. And the financial reality is that they have to be supported by what you refer to as the tripe, if we're to turn a profit.'

'But why publish the tripe at all? Why not just concentrate on the good stuff? And that stuff you like, and that Minty's always pushing - it's disgusting, mind-destroying garbage.'

'Sally, I would really like you to try to be nicer to Araminta, if it's at all possible.'

'Why?'

'Well, because it's better in all respects to be nice to people. It creates a better working atmosphere, for one thing.'

'Okay, I'll be especially nice to her from now on. In fact I'll be so nice that she'll probably be completely disconcerted and confused to the extent that she'll lose her magical touch in choosing the worst kind of tripe to peddle. Which will mean she'll become so incompetent and probably incontinent that even you'll be forced to sack her. Which will mean I won't have to look at her stupid red face any more.'

'You don't have to be that nice to her.'

'Okay, Freddy, moderation in all things, eh? Anyway, Pippa's already given me this lecture.'

'You know, she hasn't always had an easy life.'

'Who?'

'Araminta.'

'Oh, I can well believe it.'

'I know she sometimes hides her true feelings behind a hard, protective shell.'

'I'm sorry, Freddy, I'm afraid I refuse to believe that anyone who reads and promotes and claims to enjoy that trash can actually have any feelings worthy of the name.'

'That's unfair, Sally. And as far as Araminta's concerned there is a particular reason, in fact a tragic event in her past which may explain why she takes a fairly pragmatic approach to life.'

'That's very delicately expressed, Freddy. Well, what is it?'

'She lost her father at quite a young age - twelve or thirteen, I think.'

'Really? I didn't know.'

'Yes, he died in an accident.'

'Oh, that's terrible. Poor Minty. Car accident?'

'No...in fact it was a traction engine.'

Sally burst out laughing.

'You are joking, aren't you?'

'No, I'm afraid not. Apparently he'd just finished restoring a large agricultural engine - he was an engineer by profession, and a steam enthusiast in his spare time. He was on his way with a friend to a steam rally. It was the first outing for the machine since he'd finished restoring it. Unfortunately he'd chosen a route which included a long incline. So, they got halfway up this hill and realised the engine wouldn't reach the top. Now, the thing is, with these types of machine you can't change gear on the move. So they had to stop, chock the wheels, and put it in a lower gear. At some point Araminta's father was behind the engine - I think his friend was trying to restart it - her father was trying to take the chocks out - or maybe he'd just done so, I don't know. Anyway, it seems that unbeknown to him, the machine started to roll backwards, and...well, you can imagine the rest.'

There was silence for a few moments while Sally contemplated this horror.

'Well,' she said at last, 'that's a horrible thing to happen. And, of course, I'm terribly sorry.'

'So you see, Sally, that in relation to this real and tragic event in her life, the make-believe violence in the thrillers and crime stories don't really make much impression on her.'

'What you're saying is that she's been effectively and permanently desensitised.'

'No, that's not what I mean.'

'That's exactly what you're saying. And though I feel sympathy for her, of course, it doesn't alter my reasons for objecting to the kind of books you and she like so much. They're still the same old wretched mind-numbing rubbish.'

'They sell, Sally. In the final reckoning I'm a businessman, and I have to ensure that what we publish sells.'

'That's exactly the point I was making at the meeting this morning when we were discussing My so-called Big Secret! Have you looked at that thing, by the way?'

'No, not yet. Pippa's asked me to have a quick look at it.'

'My Big Secret! My Big Money-Spinning Load of Arse! more like it. It's just typical, totally typical of its type. Even the suave and attractive Daniel agreed, bloody useless though he is! In every single book of that ilk there's the obligatory young, attractive woman who is scatty and disorganised and works in publishing or journalism or PR, overspends wildly, lusts after clothes, especially fab and gorgeous underwear from Prada, Karen Millen or Ralph Lauren, doodles flowers when she's meant to be writing important reports, has quirky and eccentric parents on the verge of separation, loveable girly flat mates and their various boyfriends with names like Tarquin and Mungo, Casper and Sebastian, interminable details of their sex lives and who's shagging who - oh, and yes she's hopelessly bad at cooking, and yes she's loveably disorganised, and yes she overspends wildly and on and on and on and round and round in circles - aaaargh! Please Freddy! They're all so cute and girly and feminine and predictable! I swear I'll kill and dismember the perpetrator of the very next chick lit submission! At least that would please you and Minty!'

Freddy was smiling, enjoying the performance.

'Oh, you haven't heard the worst yet. The worst thing about them is her boyfriend. The tall, grave, tanned, incredibly important and successful hero, with his blue eyes and wavy brown/blonde hair, who makes the heroine flush, blush, turn red/crimson, her cheeks grow hot, her heart race, behave like a little girl, pant, giggle and, in extremis, tears stream down her cheeks. Later, of course, she might occasionally be brave and defiant, within certain strictly defined limits, by which time I've puked my guts out, unfortunately, and therefore lost interest in this little postfeminist romance! His hard, rough masculine skin, his muscular chest and strong forearms! Oh my God! Save me Freddy! Please, save me, with your rough, tall, strong, grave chest and forearms - save me!'

Freddy was now laughing, and he held out his arms towards Sally, who just shook her head and smiled.

'Look, I haven't read My Big Secret! yet, Sally, so I can't comment on that specifically. But they're not all so badly written really. You know they're not. And it's just escapism, anyway. They're not intended to be anything profound, or works of art. They're just something that somebody can pick up and for a few hours, without any great effort or involvement, be taken outside their own life into another world, where the characters might have problems that the reader may be able to relate to. They're not trying to be, or claiming to be, any more than they are - which is simply light, escapist, romantic fiction.'

'I just want to read about more than bloody synthetic relationships, and who's shagging who among non-characters I couldn't give a damn about. There's not one idea between the whole collection of cardboard cut-outs in the whole anthology of this godforsaken genre. And they might at least do us all a favour and keep it short, but they all drag on forever, as if they're in fact doing us a favour by demonstrating their inexhaustible paucity of imagination. And I especially hate it when they have kids, and then the kids start to do the baby talk - I lub you mummy! Dat not wot I wat, dat wot I wat! Gib oo dat me! Please, Freddy! I'm begging you! Please don't make me read any more of it! My brain can't take any more of the scatter-brained and lovable who spend too much, drink too much, relieve their angst with chocolate and pizza, date the wrong kind of guy, buy sexy underwear to impress the wrong kind of guy - and believe me, he is the wrong kind of guy, and yes of course he looks like Hugh Grant, and of course he flutters his improbably long eyelashes and laughs sardonically, and is inconsiderate and a pig, and of course we love it because we all love a bad guy that makes us all hot and excited and damp in all the right places and...'

Here she released a long scream of anguish, and threw her pen at Freddy's head. Luckily, it missed.

'Sally,' said Freddy gently, 'please don't take this the wrong way, but have you got a boyfriend at the moment?'

She looked nonplussed for just a split second.

'Get out! Get out, Freddy! I'm busy!'

7

Simon was bored and fretting in the air-conditioned cell he shared with Hugo. He'd spent some time playing various games with some marbles he kept in a drawer of his desk. Now he was trying to see how close to the edge of his desk he could roll a pencil without it falling off. The repeated rattle of the pencil across the desk was the only noise in the office apart from the hum of the air-conditioning. Hugo, trying to immerse himself in some complicated contract, and by now thoroughly distracted, laid aside his papers and regarded his friend thoughtfully.

'Simon, there's something I've been meaning to say to you for some time. And perhaps now that time has come.'

Simon looked across questioningly, and began twirling the pencil between his fingers.

'For someone like me, the generation and accumulation of wealth is all I may reasonably aspire to. But for you, Simon, with your cast of mind, I feel there is the potential for so much more - in fact, nothing less than artistic endeavour and aesthetic conquest. In short, the world is your virgin warehouse, crammed full of perfumed conceits and exotic follies, enamelled delights and scented deceptions. The sensual pleasures of opaque misinterpretation, and the seminal occlusions of mistaken insight. I envy you these possibilities, I really do.'

'Your language is clearly calculated to beguile and bewitch me. You're not trying to flatter me out of a job are you, Hugo?'

'My dear fellow, I would wish you to stay here for all eternity - you know that. But you would be the first to admit, I'm sure, that you are almost nihilistically uninterested in your work.'

'To be honest, I've never taken sufficient interest in it to find out what it actually entails. Perhaps it has depths of which I shall remain forever unaware.'

'Perhaps it has. We shall probably never know.'

'No, probably not. Are you saying that I should move on of my own free will?'

'Before you're sacked, you mean? Yes, I think that's probably a good idea. It would definitely look better on your CV.'

'Has somebody said something to you?'

'There have been certain whisperings and rumours. Of course, there always are. And knowing that we're friends, there's been nothing overt. But I think the general gist is that if you don't start to actually do something, and make some money, you're on your way out.'

'The writing on the wall is as subtle as that, is it?'

'Nothing was underlined, let's put it that way. But there was nevertheless no need to delve too deeply between the lines.'

'Or, presumably, read the small print.'

'Simon, I'm serious. What are you going to do about your future?'

'For the moment, Hugo, I'm going to completely sidestep the issue. And instead tell you about my dear old uncle.'

'What about him?'

'Don't sound so disinterested. You didn't know him like I did.'

'I didn't know him at all. What of it?'

'In fact, Hugo, what I have to tell you might actually shed some light on why I am unable to take this job seriously. My uncle - my late uncle - let's call him Uncle Gerald, for the sake of argument - anyway, my uncle had a theory, a notion, if you like, which I believe has considerable merit. He believed that - '

'I don't believe you have an uncle.'

'Of course I have an uncle. Why should I not have one? It's quite a normal sort of thing to have. Anyway, to continue, my uncle believed that - '

'Well, either he isn't dead, or else he never existed in the first place.'

'The two are hardly compatible. And I would like to make it quite clear that the times I spent with my uncle are some of my happiest childhood memories. And even if he hadn't existed, I'm sure we'd have spoken of many things, and most of those would almost certainly have been of no value at all. Anyway, as I was nearly saying, my dear old uncle believed that - '

'This mythical uncle of yours. I suppose he was quite the philosopher.'

'I believe he did have a certain way with words. Though he did once say that obfuscation and opacity were the last refuge of the emotional deviant. I assume he wasn't talking about himself.'

'He said that, this increasingly mythical uncle?'

'I keep telling you, he wasn't mythical at all, except in the allegorical sense. He was as real as you or I - well, me anyway. And yes, he really said that. My uncle was a fearless man except in times of minimal danger. Anyway, to put it as succinctly as possible, my non-mythical uncle believed that...'

Hugo picked up the mobile from his desk and looked at it pensively. Simon, perched on the edge of his own desk, studied his friend with compassion.

'I see you have your mobile back, Hugo.'
'Yes.'
'Where was it?'
'Pippa says she found it in the house.'
'So?'
'That she claims to have found it suggests that it was lost in the first place - a source of some contention.'

'That it was lost, or that she claims to have found it?'

'I don't believe it was lost. And how can you find what was never lost?'

'People find love every day, or claim to do so, and to suggest that love found is also invariably love lost would be quite perverse. Perhaps misplaced is a better word?'

'I never misplace my mobile. It is central to who I am. It would be like suggesting I'd misplaced my personality.'

'Except that would presuppose there was something to misplace in the first place, whereas your ownership of a mobile is beyond dispute.'

Hugo glared.

'Dear old Hugo,' said Simon, smiling. 'You're in danger of losing your sense of humour, surely one of your three greatest remaining assets, together with your looks and that elusive personality. To lose one, and to have a question mark hanging over another, would be to place an almost intolerable burden on the third.'

'I wish you would talk sense occasionally, Simon. I'm certain Pippa has read some messages on my phone. And I'm extremely worried about it.'

'Why are you so certain? And why does it matter? Oh, is this why you think Pippa's going cold on you - because she has certain suspicions about you?'

'She was behaving distantly towards me before I lost my phone. Though I suppose she could have read them before and then just…oh God, what a mess! What a nightmare!'

With his elbows on the table, he buried his face in his hands.

'What are these messages you're referring to? I assume they're in some way compromising?'

'Oh, judge for yourself,' said Hugo, pushing the phone towards Simon with the back of a hand.

Simon studied the relevant texts intently, glancing at his friend several times, before handing the mobile back to Hugo.

'Hmm. Nicely written. But literary merit aside, I really wouldn't worry unduly. It's clearly the work of some lunatic. That is unless you've been up to something without telling me.'

'Of course I haven't. I don't even know who's sending me these damned messages.'

'That's just what I was going to ask you. You have no idea who this person might be?'

'None whatsoever.'

'Clearly an emotional and passionate individual - about you, at any rate.'

'Please - don't remind me!'

'She has a definite way with words - the shorthand of texting, at any rate. And an unusually vivid imagination. Well, I say she - you don't suppose…'

'No, I don't!'

'No, quite. I take your point. And you say Pippa has read these messages?'

'Well, she made such a song and dance about the mobile being turned off when she gave it back to me - saying she'd just found it somewhere. She was clearly lying. Which means she must have read those texts, and consequently thinks I'm having an affair.'

'Well, did you speak to her about them?'

'No, of course not. How could I?'

'How could you? How could you not? If you really think she's read those messages then all manner of unpleasant thoughts will be racing through her mind. For God's sake, Hugo, it's a question of basic humanity!'

'It's not as simple as that. As I've told you before, there's such a distance between us at the moment that neither of us seems capable of discussing anything remotely personal. This great unspoken divide has opened up, and neither of us knows why - well, I don't anyway - or how to bridge it.'

'You communicate, for God's sake! You talk to each other! It's really not that complicated. Look, you're assuming that Pippa has read those texts on your mobile, and from that she's deduced that you're having a wild, in fact quite athletic, affair.'

'Steady on, Simon.'

'Sorry, Hugo. I forgot you don't like that sort of thing. So, on the one hand she's assuming you're having this affair.'

'I keep telling you, I'm not having it.'

'And then you've told me you have similar suspicions of her because she no longer shows any interest in you. Now, to what extent cause and effect are intertwined here, I don't know - that would depend on the timing of certain events, difficult to establish beyond question. But what is absolutely vital is, firstly, that you open the lines of communication. Try to put your pride and wounded feelings to one side for a moment and simply tell her the truth. The great beast of the jungle must for once sheath its claws, lick its wounds, and try to avoid twitching its tail in irritation.'

'That doesn't sound anything like me.'

'Secondly, we need to establish the identity of your communicant, and ask them politely to stop.'

'It's stalking, Simon, plain and simple.'

'Perhaps she's an old flame. Have you dumped anyone recently, Hugo?'

'Of course I haven't. I've been married to Pippa for years.'

'Don't make it sound like a prison sentence. It sets entirely the wrong tone. Perhaps this woman's a voice from your past. Have you got a past, Hugo?'

'Of course I haven't got a past! How can I have a past when it looks very much as though I haven't got a future?'

'Oh, paradoxes are of no use to us here. And I think you must be prepared to search your memory for anyone, anyone at all, that you may have disappointed in the past, and is now attempting, with some success, I must say, to destabilise you. Love lost, or love spurned, can result in the release of some very powerful emotions.'

Simon struck a pose, and began declaiming.

'They flee from me that sometime did me seek,
With naked foot stalking in my chamber:
I have seen them gentle, tame, and meek,
That now are wild, and do not once remember
That sometime they have put themselves in danger

> *To take bread at my hand; and now they range,*
> *Busily seeking with a continual change.*

'There, I think that says it all.'

Hugo blew out his cheeks.

'You're not helping at all, Simon. Now, you are coming tonight, aren't you?'

'Do you really want me to come?'

'Of course I really want you to come. You said you would kindly observe Pippa, and see if you could detect any unusual signs of normality.'

'That isn't quite what I said.'

'Well, come anyway. Please. There'll be someone there who might interest you.'

'Apart from you, you mean, Hugo?'

'Yes, apart from me. One of Pippa's colleagues, a young woman called Sally. I don't think you've met her before. She's extremely pretty, and also highly intelligent and unconventional. I'm sure you'll like her.'

'Fine. But even if I do like her, what am I supposed to talk to her about? I don't know anything about fashionable clothes or nail varnish or mini-breaks or cellulite, and I haven't taken the course in men-are-pointless-scum as yet.'

'Just wing it. You'll be fine. Anyway, as I say, she's not like all the rest. Talk to her about books.'

'I don't know anything about books.'

'A career in publishing awaits you. In any case, what about all the poetry you quote?'

'The ability to memorise a few lines of poetry hardly qualifies me to work in the publishing profession, or for making intelligent conversation with someone who does.'

'Well, never mind. I'm sure you'll think of something, on both counts. So we'll see you tonight?'

'Oh God, if you insist!'

8

The lamps were lit as the guests arrived. The knives, forks and spoons glittered. The glasses shone. And from this promising beginning, and up to a certain point, the dinner party was a complete success. Whatever it was that Pippa and Hugo had placed on the table had been consumed, without pause or recrimination, by their guests. And both before and throughout much of the meal, Sally had taken great pains to be exquisitely polite to Araminta, to the latter's discomfort and suspicion. And now the Labouré-Roi Crémant de Bourgogne, Château de Champteloup Crémant de Loire and Domaine de Coyeux Muscat de Beaumes de Venise were playing their traditional role of tearing down barriers. Though one voice in particular - Sally's, in fact - seemed to require neither catalyst nor encouragement.

'And certainly we should severely limit the production of tripe. Two, or at most three novels per author is quite sufficient. Too much publication is undignified, especially for the temperamentally untalented, and probably injurious to any moral sense. It suggests a morbid ambition quite out of place with the selfless egotism of the true artist.

'And these people are artists, believe me! Artists in the mould of Sam Katzman, presiding genius of Katzman quickies. In fact, the tripe we peddle reminds me very much of the old formula Elvis movies. Less creative, it's true, but similar in terms of the endless repetition of motifs. In every Elvis flick you had the babes, with plenty of lingering ass shots, the mindless violence, the cars/boats/helicopters, the insipid songs, and Elvis himself, looking uneasy and bored with the whole affair. And that's another thing - at least you got some songs, and they were at least ostensibly different for each movie, even if they were mainly rubbish. But with the garbage we churn out you don't even get that level of variety.'

Sally once more well into her stride. The difference on this occasion was that she had an ardent admirer. Simon could hardly take his eyes off her or listen to what she had to say without feeling that she was the most wonderful and engaging creature on God's earth! And almost unthinkably for Sally, she seemed to be similarly entranced by Simon. They'd struck up an immediate and intense rapport, and only the fact that Pippa had seated them on opposite sides of the table in the hope that they might notice each other - in the event, an unnecessary precaution - could have separated them.

Pippa had introduced Sally to Simon as soon as she'd arrived, and Simon had quickly taken in her fierce, intelligent eyes and pretty features.

'By the way, darling,' said Pippa, after the initial introductions. 'I don't think I've mentioned it before, but Simon's an investment banker, like Hugo.'

Sally looked at Simon with an incurious expression.

'So I gathered. How very interesting for you.'

'It's not interesting at all. It's a complete waste of time and human potential.'

Sally's expression immediately transformed, and her eyes grew round.

'Well…why do it, then?'

'I don't think I will do it for much longer. I don't think they'll let me. I've already been told I won't qualify for any bonus this year, so that's probably the kiss of death.'

'But why do it at all if you don't like it?'

'Money. Why else would anyone do such a morally offensive job. Certainly not for aesthetic pleasure or artistic fulfilment - or any other kind of fulfilment, for that matter.'

'I…well, what would you like to do?'

'Ah! Therein lies the difficulty! There exists an unfortunate tension between anything I might wish to do and anything that I might be qualified to do. In fact, I feel that the better qualified for something I am, the less likely I am to like it.'

'And are you well qualified to be an investment banker?'

'No, but that is simply the exception that confirms the paradox.'

'You seem to be saying that you can like only what you cannot know, except in those instances where you know what you cannot like. And to know is to destroy the mystery, and with it all possible charm.'

'How perfectly expressed! I wish you could express all of my thoughts in the future - I'm sure they'd come out much clearer then than they presently exist within my own mind.'

'I'm sure nothing would give me greater pleasure than to correctly interpret your innermost thoughts.'

'I only wish I had more thoughts for you to correctly interpret. My current profession unfortunately discourages that sort of thing. It renders it ethically objectionable. In fact, any activity along those lines is severely frowned upon.'

'I'm sorry to hear that.'

'Well, you can understand it from their point of view. The unprincipled pursuit of wealth is such a delicate bloom - the merest touch of introspection and it withers and dies.'

'Well, you wouldn't like it much in publishing, then. It sounds very similar. The greater the depth of thought in a novel or the more complex the ideas, the less likely it is ever to see the light of day. I'm the only one there that reads anything but mindless junk.'

'That must be very frustrating for you.'

'It is frustrating when you have a clear idea, a clear vision of something, and yet you're prevented from pursuing that vision by the dead weight of stupidity surrounding you. Oh, hello Araminta! How lovely to see you!'

Araminta looked across the room from where she'd come in with Freddy and Pippa.

'You're looking lovely tonight! Hello, Freddy.'

Freddy smiled at Sally's friendly greeting.

'Hello, Sally. Nice to see you.'

Freddy and Araminta looked at Simon.

'Oh, this is Simon - Hugo's friend. Simon, that's Freddy, and that's Araminta, two of my most valued colleagues.'

The three of them exchanged smiles and hellos. But there was no move by Simon to leave Sally's side to shake hands, and Freddy and Araminta carried on with Pippa into the spacious kitchen to greet Hugo.

'You were referring to your colleagues just now, I take it?' said Simon quietly.

'Yes, you could call them that. If you can call a random collection of people without intelligence, morals, judgement or taste colleagues, then yes, that's exactly what they are. Pippa is excluded from that assessment, by the way.'

'I'm not surprised. Pippa's one of the best.'

'She is, though not quite at her best at the moment.'

'You're aware of the mobile phone issue, then, are you?'

'The texts, you mean? I told Pippa they don't signify or prove anything.'

'Just what I indicated to Hugo. The work of some rather strange and vindictive individual intent on unsettling poor old Hugo. Worrying, of course, but not in itself cause to - '

'Would you all like to take a seat at the table now!'

Pippa's voice, high and slightly strained.

'There are place cards there for all of you - forgive our pretensions!'

The first course arrived promptly on the heels of the JP Chenet Sparkling Brut, and the two young people were forced to defer further intimate discussion - and, still more reluctantly, submit to separation by the width of a table. But there were certain compensations - as the evening progressed, Sally became more and more voluble on the subject of tripe, and Simon fell ever more deeply in love.

'And the heroine is always having these lovable, girly daydreams about winning the lottery and buying a house in Mayfair and having an incredibly important job, and she's always saying cool and fab and all the bestest and mostest funny, lovable, endearing, girly things, while her tall, grave, sardonic boyfriend gravely and sardonically patronises and belittles her, and she looks up at him and laps it all up with her little thumping heart and flushed cheeks, and in the end, she has to end up playing the little girl - giggling a lot, and swooning at the masterful authority of the tall, grave, handsome hero. Now,' said Sally, pausing dramatically, 'I don't want to descend to Minty's level of mindless animal violence, but on the other hand I shouldn't be forced to endure such provoking tripe! For the love of bollocks sake, have women moved so little forward since they were so graciously awarded the vote? Do we still have to behave like little girls to avoid being labelled harridans, dykes or ball-breakers? Why is everyone in the world so STUPID!!'

'Darling,' said Pippa, 'don't you think you're going ever so slightly over the top?'

'Slightly?' said Araminta. 'You don't believe in taking any chances, do you Pippa.'

'Plus, every other sentence starts with plus. Which would annoy the fuck out of anyone. Especially me. Plus, if anyone does it again, I'm afraid I shall be forced to…okay…okay…I can handle that. Oh yes! Plus bursting into tears! Plus, if anyone even thinks of saying yummy or prezzy or goody or hon or spritzing - especially spritzing - in any context or for any reason, even if they haven't opened their mouth, I will know. I WILL KNOW AND I WILL HAVE TO KILL! Is that okay with you, Minty? I don't want to offend your sensibilities. By the way, that's a lovely perfume you're wearing! What is it? I really must get some.'

Sally glanced innocently at Pippa and Freddy, to be greeted by frowns and slight shakes of the head.

'What? I'm being nice!'

'Why doesn't anyone ever say anything to her? Am I the only one who isn't afraid of her?'

'What's your problem?' said Sally.

'Araminta,' said Freddy, his voice gentle and calming. 'Sally and I had a lovely chat the other day, and she told me she really respects your work and wants the two of you to get on much better.'

'That is simply not the case, Freddy, and you know it. She has no respect whatsoever for the kind of work I deal with, as she's made clear on numerous occasions. And we all have to defer to her and tiptoe around her violent opinions.'

'Have we not had this discussion, or one very similar, many times before?' said Freddy, smiling.

'Discussion? What discussion? It's all Sally making her usual play to the gallery, and as usual we're stuck here having to listen to her.'

'Don't let me detain you,' said Sally. 'Feel free to go, if you've finished eating at last.'

Araminta scowled, involuntarily looking down with pink cheeks at the large slice of strawberry cheesecake on her plate.

'Anyway, this whole little girl thing. Is it just a case of sexual thrills? Is it really as primitive as that? Do such women get their kicks out of being dominated by their tall, dark, stern master? Their Darcy, their Rochester, their Luke Brandon, for Christ's sake? Is it all a glorious, illicit, spine-tingling, knee-trembling, unreconstructed, un-PC thrill for all these Sophies and Cecilias and Rebeccas? What a bunch of revolting, silly c…'

'Sally, please,' said Pippa. 'Let's keep our invective within sustainable limits.'

'I wasn't going to say what you think I was going to say. That was in your mind. Do you understand now how polluted our minds are by all the filth they're subjected to?'

'Hear, hear!' said Hugo. 'Let's talk only of what is good and pure and decent! Let's talk about Michael Schumacher!'

'Fab! Gorgeous! Scrumptious!'

'Sally, stop it.'

'Don't you think you're protesting a little too much, Sally?' said Araminta, her pretty features red and hostile. 'Are you sure you're not suffering from some repressed, and therefore inverted, desire to be in just that kind of situation?'

'No, really!' said Hugo. 'Why don't we play a variant of that old perennial, the greatest ever whatever or top twenty of whoever it might be? Racing drivers in this case. How about it? The greatest post-war racing drivers, and you're only allowed two per decade. And they have to be the quickest of the quick!'

'Right,' said Simon, jumping in on cue, 'you're on! And appropriately enough, I'm going for a banker to start off - 1950s, Fangio.'

'Wise choice, can't argue with that. And sticking with that decade, I'll go for Moss.'

'Fair enough. But what about Ascari? Some say he was quicker than Fangio.'

'Just a moment, Simon. I did stipulate only two per decade. You're already trying to flout the rules.'

'I thought that was entirely consistent with the ethos of the sport.'

'Perhaps. But to deviate briefly from small print and grey areas, I've just had a thought myself. Late 1940s - Jean-Pierre Wimille.'

'Mm. Sneaky, and a little obscure. Tell you what, I'll do a trade with you. You give me Ascari, and you can have Wimille.'

'Okay, okay. But in return, I'm going to throw you a curve ball. 1970s. Of course, Peterson, no discussion.'

'Given.'

'But here's one for you - to go with Ronnie, I want Tony Brise.'

'Good Heavens! You've got some chutzpah, I'll say that for you! But what about the likes of Stewart, Lauda, Hunt, Villeneuve, Pryce, Depailler?'

'My stipulation was for the quickest of the quick - that is the very biggest talents. Not necessarily the most successful or - '

'For God's sake,' cried Pippa, 'do we have to talk about racing drivers nobody's ever heard of? Can't we talk about something else?'

Eyes turned nervously to Pippa.

'I'm sorry,' said Hugo. 'Are we to be restricted only to racing drivers that everybody's heard of? Or do we accept a majority verdict?'

'I don't want to talk about racing drivers at all, whether I've heard of them or not.'

'I was just trying to broaden the scope of conversation, darling,' went on Hugo. 'Not that the scope of conversation was in any way restricted before, my love. Apart from the fact that it was restricted almost entirely to literature and publishing. As I say, apart from that minor proviso, the conversation was wide-ranging and eclectic.'

'It's always the same when Sally's involved,' said Araminta abruptly. 'Everything always descends into chaos and acrimony.'

The table fell silent.

'Well, that's nice,' said Sally. 'Here was I minding my own business, and also trying especially hard to be nice, especially to dear old Minty, and who should launch an unprovoked personal attack on me?ABear old Minty!'

'Sally, the great feminist! She doesn't like anything that might disturb her wonderful, pure ideas, or encroach on her shining vision of pure literature. Books where nothing happens, because nobody's allowed to say or do anything nasty to anyone. God knows what they write about in her kind of book, because as far as I can see nothing ever happens!'

'That's big talk from the woman who walks a precarious tightrope between her lack of moral sense and her lack of taste! And if you knew anything about me you'd know that I'm as much a humanist as a feminist. That's if we're going to pay any attention to the meaning of words and their precise definition. Something that I imagine wouldn't concern you too much, Minty.'

'The humanist who despises humanity!'

'I don't despise humanity as such.'

'Only certain huge chunks of it. Anyway, you know as well as I do that terms like humanism and feminism don't mean anything, as it's impossible to clearly define them.'

'Well, it's true it would be difficult to convey precisely what I mean without making a long speech.'

'Which I'm sure wouldn't deter you.'

'Which of course I would be very reluctant to do.'

'Ha.'

'So I'll try to keep it as short as possible.'

'I would just like to say,' put in Simon, 'before you begin your wonderful long speech, that I myself am a feminist, and always have been.'

'Since when?' said Hugo.

'I would prefer not to specify precisely when my lifelong commitment actually began.'

'I would suggest precisely two minutes ago.'

'The scale of time becomes quite unimportant in the context of a broad canvas of strongly held beliefs.'

'As I was saying,' continued Sally, smiling across the table at Simon, 'humanism seeks a rational and moral basis for society based on a logical, analytical approach rather than on myth, superstition or received wisdom. Now, as humanism is based on logic, it will necessarily incorporate feminism.'

'Rubbish!' said Araminta, or at any rate something analogous. 'Why should it?'

'For the reasons I've just stated. Principally that no form of society sustainable without coercion can accommodate inherent and structural power imbalances. Therefore, logically, the rational and equitable philosophy of humanism will incorporate the basic feminist concept of - What was that, Araminta? - of equal rights and status for both men and women. A position perhaps best expressed in terms of anarcho-feminism, a strand of feminism - Did you say something? - opposed to hierarchy and authority in any form, as the invariable creators of division and inequity. It naturally opposes the state as a vehicle for the centralization of power, and opposes militarism as the means of protecting the entrenched interests at the centre of the state, through aggression towards its own citizens and those of politically opposed or unaligned states. So we have feminism - Now really, that's quite unnecessary, Minty - anarchism and humanism logically interlinking in the struggle against stereotypical male concepts of aggression, authority and hierarchy. Take Herland as an illustration of what I'm talking about.'

'Ugh!'

'What's Herland?' asked Simon.

'It's the most loathsome, pervasive and recurrent of Sally's many obsessions.'

'It's the finest of all utopian novels, by the writer Charlotte Perkins Gilman. She uses the medium of a society of empowered women to show that the feminine values of caring, cooperation and non-violence - That's not very polite, Minty - are the only possible basis for a peaceful and satisfying society. But these women also have the masculine virtues of firm decisiveness and physical strength. A perfect blend of what are commonly even now two opposed positions. She clearly felt that the best way of demonstrating her ideas was through an all-female society - I don't think it's necessary to use language like that - freed from the subjection of men and from the standards of societies where the meanings of masculine and feminine are exaggerated and polarised into separate and opposing experiences.'

'Garbage!' said Araminta, or something of the kind.

'Indeed it is,' agreed Sally.

'Forgive me,' said Simon, 'for asking a rather basic question - sorry Hugo - but how was this race continued without men?'

'Parthenogenesis.'

'Ah! Of course! Very handy too!'

'But the essence of the book is Gilman's belief that masculine and feminine values are not peculiar or exclusive to either gender. She believed that gender differences in behaviour are more the result of conditioning than not, and that males and females have the capacity for both masculine and feminine behaviours.'

'I hate that kind of thinking!'

'And, by inference, that in normal mixed gender human communities both men and women should adopt feminine values and behaviours as the only means to a peaceful and cooperative society.'

'God, what utter rubbish!' said Araminta, once again indulging in euphemism, and with a disgusted flick of her immaculately conditioned hair.

'And literature has a vital role to play in changing perceptions such that progress towards this society becomes possible.'

'Literature reduced to moral tract!'

'Darling,' said Pippa hastily, 'I know this fictional society and this race of women with their great purity of mind have become an ideal for you. But don't you think it a tad unrealistic? I mean, how do you in day-to-day life tread that line between fiction and reality? How do you keep to the purity of your own ideals in an imperfect world? It's all very well keeping this ideal in mind, but how do you avoid becoming an island?'

'Sally has such contempt for humanity that that's hardly an issue,' said Araminta. 'A strange stance for a self-confessed humanist!'

'What I meant,' said Pippa hastily, 'was that only by recognising, facing, exposing yourself to the reality of human behaviour can you do something about changing it. Surely this is the best route to rationality. Otherwise you lose yourself in impossible ideals, like Herland. Surely we have to - in literature especially - confront our own failings. If we just deny them, is there not a risk of driving our elemental, primal natures underground?'

'Well, that's where we differ, Pippa. I don't regard the so-called dark side of human nature as elemental. I see it, as did Gilman, as essentially learned and imitative.'

'Sally, darling, I honestly think you have to make a choice: become a pure, inviolable island, or risk tainting your purity by engaging with reality.'

'And as an example of what I'm talking about,' said Sally, roundly ignoring Pippa's observation, 'I managed to get through Bridget Jones's Diary' - her voice conveyed profound disapproval - 'without actually throwing up. Of course, sadly it became the Blue Hawaii to the whole rotten genre. But what was really offensive was its bastard offspring - that film!' Here her voice became grim, almost vicious. 'It is simply the most cynical and disgusting thing I have ever seen! That fight scene. It wasn't in the book. It was stuffed into the film, surely the most cynical touch of the whole sordid business. Why was that thought suitable for a light romantic comedy - or for any piece of entertainment, for that matter?'

There was some laughter at this. But not from Simon, now entirely consumed with love and admiration, his eyes shining. Nor from Pippa, whose expression betrayed concern. Knowing better than anyone how sincere and strongly held were Sally's beliefs.

'Well I don't care what you say. Thrillers, crime novels, romantic comedies - they're the genres that sell in big numbers. They're the books that make real money and keep publishers in business. Ask Freddy. Ask any publisher. Ask any literary agent, for that matter.'

'Literary agents? Those illiterate, licentious insects!'

'Did you say insects or incests?' asked Simon, smiling.

'Insects, incests, it's all the same! They're drones, clones, worms, parasites! They're lizards, they're egg-eaters, they're vermin! They're mud-burrowers and nest-stealers! In fact, they're nothing, by definition. They create nothing, they contribute nothing. I don't listen to anything any agent has to say. Ever. I hope I've made myself sufficiently clear.'

'You have, and yet I'd love to hear it all again,' said Simon. 'It was quite wonderful!'

'I never repeat myself,' said Sally, 'nor do I give encores. To experience the unrepeatable is to walk with angels, whereas repetition invites ennui, and is therefore incompatible with sublimity. I thought I'd already made that concept quite clear, and I'd be reluctant to repeat myself, for obvious reasons.'

'We'd all be even more reluctant if you did,' put in Araminta.

'Your repetition,' replied Simon, 'would contain more that was truly original than the most newly-minted insight of poet or philosopher.'

'For God's sake,' burst out Araminta. 'This is becoming nauseous.'

'Well,' said Pippa, reacting swiftly to avert unpleasantness, 'why don't we leave the table now, and just chat and relax. Sally, would you like to give me a hand? No, no,' she said hurriedly, as other hands moved to help, 'we'll manage. Please just leave the table and go and relax. We'll manage perfectly well.'

9

Freddy was describing his large luxury property to Araminta, beginning with the beautiful grounds approaching eight acres incorporating ornamental ponds, stone terraces, stables (with tack room), paddocks (with windbreaker), useful outbuildings, productive vegetable and soft fruit garden, and of course formal mature gardens. Proceeding inside the striking 17th. century six-bedroom property, Freddy drew attention to the four large reception rooms, and also the retention of many period features including porch, oak panelling and exposed beams. Needless to say, Araminta was spellbound, such that she hardly noticed Sally and Pippa clearing the table.

Across the room by the windows stood Simon and Hugo, conversing in hushed tones.

'Have you spoken to Pippa yet?' asked Hugo in a low voice.

'No, not yet Hugo. I haven't really had an opportunity yet.'

'I'm not surprised. Your eyes have been more or less permanently glued to Sally.'

'That's a ridiculous slander!'

Simon turned, and watched as Sally collected plates and cutlery. His expression became hungry and intense, and his eyes followed her from the room. Then he turned slowly back to Hugo.

'Is it really that obvious?'

'I'm afraid so.'

'But she is so extraordinary!'

'Yes, I know.'

'She is absolutely wonderful!'

'Yes, she is.'

'She is so wondrously beautiful!'

'I know, and in so many ways.'

'She has the most stunning intellect of any woman I've ever met!'

'A partial yet undeniable opinion.'

'I've never met anybody like her!'

'No, I don't suppose you have.'

'I could never love anybody else!'

'No, I suppose not.'

'Tell me what I should do, Hugo.'

'Yes, you're quite right.'

'What was that?'

'Oh, I'm sorry, Simon. My mind was wandering.'

'I was asking you what I should do about Sally. Do you think I should ask her to marry me straight away? Do you think she'd say yes?'

'I don't think there is anything to be done. I think it may be a lost cause.'

'What?'

'I just don't think…oh, I apologise, Simon. My mind was straying once again. Look, I really don't think I'm qualified to give you advice on women, given the perplexities of my present domestic situation.'

'You mean you're still in the soup with Pippa?'

'In a nutshell - yes.'

'She does seem a little on edge. Have you spoken to her?'

'Repeatedly.'

'I mean have you spoken to her recently?'

'Often.'

'I mean about the lack of communication?'

'No.'

'Or whether she looked at the texts on your mobile?'

'No.'

'Or about how much you love her?'

'No.'

'Ah. In that case I think I may have identified the problem. I think your extraordinary wit and sparkling loquacity is simply overwhelming her. Tone it down a little, Hugo. Give her time to formulate some satisfyingly inadequate and unconvincing responses.'

'This is no laughing matter, Simon. I tell you, she simply refuses to communicate with me. Talking to her these days is like trying to hold a conversation with an answering machine, and about as rewarding.'

'Yes, I can imagine that feeling.'

'You saw what she was like - behaving very strangely.'

'I thought she was behaving entirely normally - if a little tense. Which is quite understandable, considering the maelstrom of suspicion and fear that must presently constitute her state of mind.'

'She should have faith in me. She should know that I would never have an affair, never cheat on her. She should put her faith in me.'

'Should? Should? People don't always do or think what we think they should! Stop thinking about should, and think instead of love, care, compassion, human frailty. Pippa is a normal, fallible, faithful, kind, caring person. Given to all the normal range of doubts and fears, hopes and regrets. Stop thinking about should, and reach out, without judgement or expectation. Reach out in a spirit of caring generosity.'

'I thought you said she was a woman.'

'She is a woman. What of it?'

'And twice in reference to my wife you've used the word normal.'

'Have I? What about it?'

'You're asking me to behave in a calm, rational, generous manner to someone you once defined as being generically insane. Yet now is apparently normal.'

'I'm asking you to suspend your instinct for sweeping generalisations. Take me as your model.'

'You? The man who would take any and every random event and sweep them all into some general theory if it suited your purpose!'

'Flexibility! Let that be your watchword, Hugo. Be constrained no longer by rigid dogma. For too long you have had - excuse my candour - a somewhat predictable approach to philosophical issues. Cast aside such narrow precepts. Remember - rules exist only as working models, to be adapted, modified and finally put aside in the face of new evidence.'

'Your infatuation with Sally wouldn't have anything to do with this miraculous conversion, would it?'

'And Sally, as you suggest, exists as evidence that woman can be wonderfully, gloriously, miraculously sane! Better than sane! Woman as artist, as visionary! Transforming our perceptions, expanding our possibilities, transcending our sanity!'

'For God's sake, Simon!'

'All our lives we've believed that what we think is normal, acceptable, logical - in a word, sane.'

'We?'

'And we were completely wrong! Don't you see that now? Everything that we accepted as normal was mere childish self-indulgence. Sally has redefined the parameters of sanity!'

'How much wine have you had tonight?'

'We were simply foolish, ignorant and muddle-headed! Who's sane now, Hugo? Who displays reason, judgement, sense, vision? Sally has revealed my insanity, and by doing so rendered me sane! And my world - our world - is changed forever!'

'I'm going to marry him.'

'What?'

'I said, I'm going to marry him.'

'Keep your voice down. There's no surer way of putting a man off than by getting all intense and serious almost the first second you meet him.'

'God, just listen to yourself! What would you have me do, Pippa? Play hard to get? Pretend I don't care? You really don't know me, do you.'

'Sally, don't you understand, you need time to get to know somebody. Of course we all like Simon very much - that goes without saying. But both of you need time to really get to know each other, and to understand your true feelings.'

'I love him! I will never love anyone else as long as I live! He is the man I have always dreamed about, and if he feels the same way about me as I do about him - and I am pretty certain that he does - then we shall certainly be married!'

'Pippa…'

Pippa turned abruptly at the sound of Hugo's voice. Her face drained of colour and her hands trembled.

'Hugo! How long have you been standing there?'

'I've just walked into the room. What on earth's the matter?'

'Nothing…nothing at all. What do you want?'

Hugo was silent for a moment, perplexed and unhappy.

'Freddy's having to leave, and Araminta's going with him. You'll want to say goodbye.'

'Why are they going now? I thought we were all going to sit down and relax. And we haven't even had coffee yet.'

'Apparently you're having a meeting first thing tomorrow. I…'

He stopped abruptly.

'I'll just go and say goodbye,' said Sally, quietly putting down her tea towel, leaving Hugo and Pippa looking searchingly into each other's face.

'Well,' said Sally at last.

'Well,' repeated Araminta coldly.

Freddy smiled, while Simon watched with a more anxious half-smile from over by the window.

'Well,' said Sally once again, 'I enjoyed our little chat today.'

'Yes, so did I.'

'We must do it again some time.'

'Yes,' agreed Araminta, pouting, 'we must.'

Pippa came through from the kitchen.

'We've had a wonderful time,' said Araminta, turning her back on Sally. 'Thank you.'

'So you two are off, then?'

'Yes,' said Freddy. 'Sorry to rush off, Pippa. I'm giving Araminta a lift back to her flat. And I'd like to call a meeting first thing tomorrow, if that's okay?'

Sally and Simon's eyes were fixed on each other, their bodies close. Simon's voice was hushed, almost whispering.

'Your friend Araminta has a surprisingly good mind.'

'Indeed she does. Such a good mind, in fact, that she uses it quite sparingly. For fear of wearing it out, presumably.'

Simon laughed.

'It's such a shame you don't get on.'

'Who says we don't get on?'

'I thought the evidence spoke for itself.'

'Never trust evidence that speaks for itself. It has a nasty habit of misrepresenting its intentions.'

With a final smile and wave from Freddy, he and Araminta left the room with Hugo. Pippa, rather than following her guests to the door, looked across at Simon and Sally.

'Sally, could I borrow you for a moment, please?'

She turned and walked through to the kitchen. Sally smiled at Simon, and squeezed his hand.

'Won't be a minute. I think I've been a bad girl again.'

'A spanking?'

'Oh, a spanking at the very least, I should think!'

In the kitchen Pippa turned and looked evenly at Sally.

'Sally, I really think you should be a little more circumspect in showing how much you like him.'

'Do you?'

'Well, it's embarrassingly obvious.'

'Is it?'

'Yes, I'm afraid it is.'

'Well, I'm sorry Pippa. Especially as now he's going to come back to my flat and probably spend the night there!'

'You surely don't mean you're going to have sex with him? You've only just met!'

'That's a bit of a personal question, Pippa. And the answer's probably yes.'

'I don't know what to say.'

'Sex can be beautiful with the right person, if memory serves me correctly. So why should we not have sex straight away?'

'But not on the very first day of meeting someone. Especially someone that you might possibly want to have a long-term relationship with, for God's sake!'

'So sex is fine so long as it's casual and meaningless, then?'

'I didn't mean that.'

'You do have sex with Hugo, don't you Pippa?'

'What's that got to do with...well, I...no, not very much at the moment, to be honest. I...I'm not sure that Hugo entirely approves of sex within marriage at the best of times. And lately...'

'Pippa, I think this all comes back to one thing. And I keep telling you, and you keep not listening. Now I'm going to tell you for the last time, so pin your ears back. Now, have you heard of emotions?'

'Yes, of course.'

'That's good. That shows we're on the right lines. Now, what are they for - what purpose do they serve?'

'I'm not sure that they serve any logical purpose as such.'

'Not quite the answer I was looking for. In fact they are the means by which we experience the extraordinary gift of life. Without emotions, the ability to feel love and joy, fear and grief, we would be mere automatons. Now, what happens if we don't express these things we call emotions?'

'I don't know.'

'Well, what happens is that, in the case of the emotion called love, the other person doesn't know how we really feel about them. And what is the probable outcome of that?'

'I don't know.'

'Misunderstandings. Crossed connections. Lost opportunities. Now, we don't want that to happen, do we Pippa?'

'No.'

'No. So what are we going to do about it?'

'We're going to express our emotions.'

'Excellent! And when are we going to expedite this intention?'

'As soon as circumstances permit.'

'No. Unfortunately, that's not the correct answer. You'd done very well up to that point. In fact we do it straight away. Now. This very minute. Or at least, as soon as Simon and I have left, which we're going to do right now, as I am experiencing a deep aesthetic desire to be alone with him in my bedroom.'

'I will try, Sally. But it isn't easy. You don't know how forbidding Hugo can be.'

'Oh, but I do. You mean so stern and masterful? Pippa, I've read about such men many, many times. And of course it's difficult for a mere woman to stand up to such an onslaught of masculinity. But we must try, and keep on trying. Don't you agree?'

'I suppose so.'

'That's my girl! Now, we must be off. See you tomorrow, Pippa!'

'Yes. And thanks, Sally.'

'No problem. Just keep that little chin up!'

10

'Simplistic and ridiculous!' said Araminta.

'Well, maybe I'm just a simplistic kind of guy,' said Freddy, a little discomfited by her reaction. 'But Araminta, don't you think there's a justifiable element of public good to be considered? Surely we - '

'Why are you suddenly coming out with this redundant argument?'

'Don't we have some civic responsibility to contribute towards a happy, peaceful society in whatever way we can? In our case that comes down to the kind of books we publish, and the content as well as quality of those books.'

'We have no responsibility beyond that of producing books that entertain people. Clearly we don't have any moral duty to hold their hands and tell them what they should or should not be reading.'

'I don't think it's a case of telling people what they should be reading, as such. It's more a question of deciding for ourselves what standards we want to set in terms of the moral content of the work we produce.'

'Have you really been taken in by Sally's pious sermonising? The essence of Western society at its best - its distinguishing feature, regardless of any flaws and failings - is freedom of speech and freedom of artistic expression. And what you seem to be suggesting is to compromise that most precious of freedoms and wilfully, voluntarily censor and circumscribe the work of our authors. I can't believe we're even discussing this.'

Freddy glanced across at Sally.

'What do you think, Sally?'

Sally was doodling on a pad - flowers, trees, a little house with single chimney, sash windows and curtains with psychedelic patterns. She looked up with a clear, happy, smiling expression.

'About what, Freddy?'

'About what we've just been talking about, of course.'

'Oh...sorry, I wasn't really listening. I agree with you...or Araminta...or Jemima...or Rebecca...or...well, it doesn't really matter which!'

'What's wrong with you, anyway?' said Araminta.

'Wrong? Nothing's wrong. In fact everything couldn't be righter!'

'Sally, haven't you been listening to what's been said?'

'You were saying something about censoring the books we publish, weren't you Freddy?'

'I didn't use the word censorship.'

'No, of course not. Censorship is such a pejorative term.'

'You don't seem to be taking this very seriously, Sally, which I find surprising.'

'Sorry, Freddy. I'll try to be more serious. Should we be censoring, I mean adjusting, certain aspects of the work we publish? Yes, of course.'

'Why, in your opinion?'

'Well, to encapsulate, I believe we have a duty as citizens to take a wider view than simply whether a certain piece of work is going to trip up on the Obscene Publications Act. Which in any case turns a completely blind eye to literature, however depraved. The authorities have conceded defeat, so it's down to the individual to take a stand.'

'I thought you were opposed to the state,' said Araminta. 'Funny then that you're bemoaning the authorities for not coming down against what you would define as an obscene novel.'

'Obscenity can mean many different things. You probably relate it simply to sexual matters and the explicit depiction of sexual practices. Which doesn't really bother me at all, as long as it's consensual and doesn't go on too long. Which if it's anything like real life, it certainly won't.' Looking wonderingly into space. 'Though there are always exceptions, of course.'

'Is there a point to any of this?'

Sally smiled.

'Yes, of course. I know, and I'm sorry. I was about to say that what does bother me is that the depiction of brutal violence, which according to case law is supposed to come within the test of obscenity, is in fact given a free ride. That's what really concerns me, and for all the reasons I tried to explain yesterday, that's what we should be looking at.'

'God, Sally, you can be very boring and repetitive sometimes!'

Though now with some appearance of conscious effort, Sally still responded with a big, welcoming smile.

'I know. And I'm sorry. I do try not to be, but I know that often I don't succeed. I know, and I'm sorry.'

'For God's sake stop saying that!'

'I know. I'm sorry. But aside from the issue of violence, I think what is most important for society is that people keep their perversions to themselves.'

'Meaning what?'

'Meaning that whatever people do behind closed doors, or in the privacy of their own mind, in public they keep up a front of civilized good manners and moral rectitude.'

'Ha! Lovely old-fashioned Victorian hypocrisy!'

'I'm a great believer in hypocrisy,' said Sally. 'So long as it's not malicious or malignant.'

'You don't actually believe in free speech or openness of expression at all, do you? You'd like everything circumscribed to your own narrow and restrictive outlook. In fact, now I think about it, you're just a fascist, Sally!'

For once the wind dropped abruptly from Sally's sails, and a deadly calm settled. Araminta's eyes gleamed.

'I…that's not true at all. I would never dream of restricting political expression, so long as…'

'I wasn't talking specifically of political expression.'

'Or the expression of any fetish, perversion or sexual quirk which doesn't involve violence that isn't consensual, or any philosophical expression, or - '

'You do like to narrow down the range of subject matter, don't you.'

'No, I've just said I don't. You aren't listening.'

'Tell us about your perversions then, Sally. Do you have many?'

'I'm sure I have as interesting a range of perversions as anyone else. And, for all you know, I may have some quite disgusting personal habits to go with them.'

'I'm sure that's not the case,' said Daniel.

'I'm not saying I necessarily do, Daniel. I'm just saying I might.'

'Tell us all about them, Sally.'

'You mean what I do 'neath the covers in the dead of night, with the rain lashing against the window pane, and the church clock striking one? What vile perversion rears its ugly head from the depths of the bed sheets, casting an ominous shadow over the dressing table? You really want to know? You want to hear every sordid detail?'

'I'm sure you don't have any perversions at all, Sally,' persisted Daniel. 'I can't imagine you having any.'

Jemima sniffed loudly several times.

'They're the worst kind. The ones you think you can trust. The ones that always take the moral high ground. They're the worst. Believe me, I know. And incidentally, if you can't imagine me having any perversions, doesn't that necessarily involve the effort of trying to imagine me attempting some disgusting practice or other, even if you then dismiss it as too extreme for someone of my moral purity to attempt? If so, I wonder which one in particular you were imagining. And how graphically you were visualising it. Let me know after the meeting if you think it might be something worth trying.'

Jemima collapsed in tears and ran from the room.

'Daniel,' said Sally, with a gesture of her head.

'Got it,' said Daniel, and went in pursuit.

'Poor woman. Still, it's having the desired effect.'

'And what about your obsession with the great disclaimer?'

'What?'

'Philip Roth. The great disclaimer and pornographer. The celebrated mask-wearer who indignantly and contemptuously and wearily and wearisomely repudiates and disclaims any validity for the uncanny symmetry of his life and that of his fictional proxies. Is there even one of his loathsome novels where we are not introduced to his penis - or rather of course the penis of one of his proxies? Or rather, have it thrust in our face, usually quite literally?'

'Congratulations! Clearly you have given his works close study. To have read so extensively and understood so little is quite remarkable.'

Araminta's colour deepened.

'Do you deny that you like his work?'

'Did I ever say that I do?'

'In several of your many speeches.'

'I don't recall. I need to have them catalogued and indexed. Then photocopied or preferably Xeroxed, then distributed to all the great thinkers throughout the world. Just to put them in their place and prove a point. After all, somebody has to be number one.'

'Like Michael Schumacher, you mean,' said Pippa brightly, through the veil of her misery.

'Yes, very much like Michael Schumacher. Though possibly minus the sublimely - or possibly subliminally - belligerent chin.'

'Roth is entirely concerned with exploring and expressing his disgusting fetishes and obsessions. And he puts them right in the shop window, and you don't seem to object to that.'

'There's nothing malicious, sadistic or deliberately exhibitionist about his work. It doesn't offend me because it's as close as you'll get to pure self-expression, though he would doubtless dispute that point. Plus, he's a great artist.'

'Plus, doesn't that rather fly in the face of your aversion to perversion?'

'No, as I've said before, so long as our perversions aren't put on public display, but kept for best in parlour, shag pile rug or even bedroom, then I have no objections at all.'

'But that's exactly what we're talking about here, for God's sake! Either you count literature as public display, or you don't. You can't have it both ways. You just haven't thought this through.'

'Araminta has a point there, Sally,' said Freddy.

'No, she hasn't got a point,' said Sally hotly. 'The difference is that Roth happens to be a great artist. Whereas I don't want to hear of any of your perversions, because none of you are remotely artists. Nor are the overwhelming majority of the deadbeats we publish.'

'So you agree that literary merit is a reasonable defence against a charge of obscenity?'

'Literary merit? The stuff we handle?'

Sally laughed, but now there was harshness in her laughter, and her eyes flashed.

'I'm asking you, do you accept that artistic merit is a defence?'

'I don't make the obscenity laws. My concern is with morality, not legality. And no depiction of violence has artistic merit, so far as I'm concerned. Is the most elegantly conceived murder or artistically portrayed execution any more aesthetically desirable or satisfying than depiction of the most commonplace brutality? Of course not. There is no beauty in violence. I don't find anything beautiful in something that offends my sense of decency and of human dignity. Anything that in the judgement of any reasonable person depraves and corrupts should be censored for the good of all - children, in particular, who need the most careful guidance, as Gilman was at pains to point out.'

Standing by the coffee machine, Jemima turned quickly to hide her face as the door creaked.

'Jemima?'

Her body stiffened at the sound of Daniel's voice.

'Jemima?' he repeated softly.

She turned.

'Oh, sorry Daniel. I didn't hear you.'

'I just came to see how you are. Is everything okay?'

'Yes, of course. I just had something…I mean, I came to get a coffee. Would you like one?'

'No, thank you.'

Her face fell.

'I mean, yes please. That would be lovely.'

He settled on a chair, pushing his glasses back to examine Jemima's thin body and straw-blonde hair.

'Sally is funny, isn't she. You can't help liking her.'

Jemima directed a sorrowful look.

'How much do you like her, Daniel?'

'How do you mean?'

'Well, I mean do you really like her?'

'It depends what you mean by really like her.'

'I mean really, really like her.'

'I wouldn't say I really, really like her.'

'You wouldn't? But still, you do like her?'

'What are you trying to say, Jemima?'

'Oh nothing. Nothing really.'

Her voice trailed away as she retrieved the coffees.

'But…but she did say she had a full range of perversions. And some disgusting habits.'

Daniel smiled.

'She was joking, Jemima.'

'Perhaps…perhaps if I had some perversions you'd find me more interesting. Perhaps you'd like me as much as her!'

The sudden emotion caused Daniel to look intently at the side of Jemima's head.

'Jemima, of course I like you as much as her - much more so, in fact. And Sally was joking. You must recognise her style of humour by now, surely?'

'Oh well, perhaps you think I'm…I'm just stupid, then. Here's your coffee, Daniel.'

'Of course I don't,' he said softly, rising to take the coffee from her, and now standing beside her. 'Quite the reverse, in fact. Thank you.'

'Do you…do you really like me as much as her if not more so, in fact. You're welcome.'

'Yes, of course I do! I've always liked you almost more than words can express. Mm, it's lovely, thanks.'

'But I always thought you really, really liked Sally and weren't even at all interested in me. It's not too hot, is it?'

'Jemima, I've always been more than interested in you. No it's just right, thanks. Of course I admire Sally tremendously for her intellect and strength of mind, but she's far too fiery for me to handle - too young and pretty as well, come to that.'

'I'm not that old. And I do have some strength of mind. And I'm sorry I'm not very pretty. It's not too sweet for you, is it?'

Moved by compassion, and afraid that she was about to do a runner again, Daniel reached out and clasped a quivering hand.

'I think you're very pretty, Jemima. More than pretty. Beautiful, in fact. No, really, it's perfect, thanks.'

'Do you really think that, Daniel?'

Her wan blue eyes were glistening. Daniel suddenly took her in his arms beside the coffee machine.

'Oh, Jemima!'

'Oh, Daniel!'

'You know what Sally thinks?'

A small, reluctant voice answered from around the second button of his shirt.

'No, I don't suppose I do.'

'She thinks we should always express our emotions - fully and openly.'

'Oh.'

They begin kissing passionately.

'I think it's really just a question of emphasis and degree as much as anything else.'

'Well, notwithstanding all Sally's strange arguments, what you are proposing is little more or less than censorship. It involves taking some ridiculous self-imposed moral stance and deciding on behalf of our readers what is good for them and what is not. I want to make it quite clear that I object to this policy absolutely and on principle.'

'Principles, Minty? Must put that one in my diary.' Araminta glared. 'Look, what you do here every day is effectively censorship. Of course you rationalise it by saying that such and such submission is not up to your high standards. What you really mean is that you don't like it, and therefore you are unable to perceive any merit in it. That's a common and understandable reaction. But let's not confuse it with any objective assessment of merit. It's censorship by the back door. You reject what you don't agree with, and square it with yourself by saying it's not up to the wonderful standards we demand here.'

'Araminta, we're not about to cut out the thrillers and crime stories. We can't afford to, and I personally don't want to. What I'm proposing is that we publish only work with implied, rather than explicit violence wherever feasible. And where sexually deviant practices are seen as inherent to the plot, they should be softened and moderated as far as possible.'

'That's ridiculous and unworkable. It would render any piece within those genres meaningless.'

'They are meaningless. What on earth is the point of them?'

'That's your opinion!'

'Whose opinion did you want?'

'Not yours, anyway!'

'That's nice, Minty! So much for freedom of speech.'

'Why don't we just see how it goes. We can all have an input into any decisions that are made.'

'Censorship by committee. What could be better.'

As the room cleared, Araminta remained seated, until at last she was alone with Freddy.

'You aren't very happy about any of this, are you.'

'What do you expect me to say? You seem to be under Sally's spell, just like everyone else.'

'I'm certainly not under any kind of spell. I'm just open to new ideas and arguments.'

'Open to the power of suggestion, you mean.'

'Araminta, if this idea proves unworkable then we'll drop it. It's as simple as that. I'm not putting the financial future of the firm on the line in any way.'

'Do you really think writers are going to accept their work being hacked around?'

'You know that most writers are open to a certain degree of editing. Many welcome it, in fact. But in any case, I see this as an opportunity to change perceptions, in our own small sphere.'

'I think it's ridiculous. And I think most writers will be able to distinguish between editing and censorship. And I feel I've been undermined, Freddy, and my position in this firm diminished. You've taken Sally's side in all of this and left me isolated. And just when I thought…'

'Araminta, you are the most important person to me in this firm, by a long, long way.'

The vulnerable tone and air of desolation had excited all of Freddy's protective instincts.

'Not just in this firm, in fact. You know that, surely, by now.'

In attempting to reply, her voice became a whisper. And Freddy could think only of the shimmering, almost translucent sheen of her hair, a variegation of various umbers, hennas and siennas. And of her swelling, womanly breasts and ample, rolling downland curves. The bangles on her wrist below the tiny, almost invisible hairs reaching up her arm, and the delicate silver bracelet watch with turquoise face resting on her pale skin. Dark, expressive eyes and pensive expression. His own long, steady loneliness, the desperate desire to recapture the illusion of forever. The scent of summer that surrounded her.

'Tell me what you're thinking, Freddy. Please.'

But there were so many thoughts, and not all were on such a pure and elevated level. In fact, some were as to the style and colour of her underwear. And some were of a conscious effort to deflect speculation as to whether she shaved 'down below' (for the record, he rather hoped she didn't). But if so, how did she cope with those troublesome 'in-between times'. But then he didn't want to entertain such thoughts at all, and fought them and berated himself fiercely for allowing their existence. But if Sally was right, and it was one of the arguments that had most impressed him, then such internalised musings were nothing to be ashamed of - were quite natural, in fact. And only their explicit externalisation was to be avoided.

And how could all that youth and beauty represent attainable reality? If he reached out would his hand pass through the image as through a phantom? Or would she turn bright red, as so often in her joustings with Sally, and slap his face, walk from the room and resign the next day? In all the confusion of unreality, which was the least unlikely?

And yet now she was beside him, and beyond the bounds of his secret yearnings they were suddenly in each other's arms. The first, exploratory embrace, and by the warmth of her body and moist fragrance of her kisses he knew the living, breathing reality beyond the image.

'You know what Sally thinks?' said Freddy at last. Araminta pulled back, yet still smiling, still holding on tightly.

'Why should I care what Sally thinks, Freddy? What on earth possessed you to bring up her name, now of all times?'

'In a strange way, I think she's brought us together.'

'That would be strange.'

'Don't you think she's sort of made it possible?'

'I don't mind. Not anymore. Not now.'

11

'I've never known you really fall for a man before, Sally.'

'There never was such a man before, Pippa! He is beyond perfect, beyond wonderful, beyond exquisite! Aesthetics are his very lifeblood, coursing with pure vigour through his veins! Morality to him is like the beating of his heart, powerful, steady and true! His purity of mind is both shield and carapace against a callous and unthinking world! Even his failings, non-existent as they are, sparkle like precious gems set in gold!'

'Did you sleep with him the other night, by the way?'

Sally smiled.

'He is quite simply perfect! Quite, quite perfect! In every conceivable way!'

'Well, Sally, I'm really pleased you like him.'

'Oh Pippa, has there ever been such untarnished goodness? Such unrivalled generosity of spirit?'

'Probably not. By the way, do you fancy another drink while we're waiting?'

'No, let's wait for them to arrive. Oh, how long are they going to be? I want to see him again! I want to touch him and hear his voice once more!'

'Hugo said they might be a few minutes late.'

Sally's expression suddenly darkened.

'Incidentally, Pippa, I must ask you something before they come. I'm not really a fascist, am I?'

'No, of course you're not, darling.'

'I don't want to be a fascist.'

'You aren't one, darling. The uniform wouldn't suit you, anyway. You're just someone with rather intolerant and uncompromising opinions.'

'Isn't that a working definition of a fascist?'

'I wouldn't put it that strongly. Chauvinist, perhaps.'

'Oh great. So if I don't quite qualify as a Nazi, I'm a flag-waving chauvinist instead.'

'Darling, you know that's not true.'

'That's what Araminta thinks.'

'Things are said in the heat of the moment, Sally. You should know that better than anybody.'

'Thanks.'

'You know what I mean.'

Sally looked closely at her friend.

'By the way, Pippa, I haven't liked to mention it, but I'm not unaware that you still seem very down. And you looked so sad yesterday as well. Have you and Hugo still not…'

'No, of course we haven't.'

'But I thought you were going to sort it all out that evening of your lovely dinner party, as I'd instructed you to.'

'I'm afraid the conversation didn't quite move in that direction.'

'I thought you were going to proactively direct it in that direction.'

'Well, I didn't. I had something on my mind.'

'What do you mean?'

Pippa's face seemed at once gaunt, her eyes haunted.

'I'm late.'

'Late? Late for what?'

'You know - late.'

'Oh, I see. Late. Right. Oh, right. Well, this complicates matters somewhat. So what have you been up to, exactly?'

'What do you think?'

'I thought you said Hugo didn't approve?'

'He doesn't. Well, sometimes you'd think he didn't.'

'So how late are you?'

'Late enough to be extremely worried. And of course it could hardly have happened at a worse time. Oh God, Sally - I don't want to end up like my parents.'

The day before the dinner party Pippa had driven down to visit. Desultory chat with her mother, resigned and querulous, picking up and putting down the TV guide, her eyes drawn more to Jeremy Kyle than her daughter. After quarter of an hour she'd managed to escape to the garage, her father greeting her with his usual tired, detached smile. Pippa looking at his latest project - Titanic, on a wooden trestle on the garage floor. Not yet complete - still awaiting masts, funnels and some superstructure. Impressive, though. Before that the Hindenburg and R101 - his airship period. Sir Thomas Bouch's Tay Bridge - doomed engine and carriages already entombed within the high girders.

'We can't see into other people's relationships, Pippa,' said Sally after Pippa had told her how she saw her parents' marriage. 'Maybe there is still love there, of a kind.'

Pippa smiled.

'And what kind could that possibly be?'

'I don't know. Not of a kind that you or I could recognise, perhaps. But then maybe nobody on the outside can do more than guess at the reality within. Presumably it still means something to them.'

'Of course it doesn't. And what if they only stayed together because of me? What if they're only still together now because of me, for God's sake?'

'Don't be so absurdly egotistical! Is such a thing really likely?'

'Is anything people do likely?'

'Not usually, but occasionally they'll catch us out with some form of explicable behaviour.'

'And what if Hugo and I find ourselves in exactly the same position, remaining together for precisely the same reason?'

'Don't worry, Pippa. People get divorced very readily these days, not infrequently involving the very youngest of children. And still less infrequently involving the very slenderest of motivations.'

'Is that supposed to make me feel better?'

'Sorry. I was only trying to help. For God's sake, I wish they'd turn that bloody thing off!'

A flat-screen television dominated one wall.

'It's only tennis, darling.'

'I don't care what it is. It's intrusive and annoying. I think I'll go and tell them to turn it down.'

'Not again, Sally - please. It was embarrassing the last time. You'll get us thrown out.'

'Well, I don't...he's here! At last! Simon! Simon, we're over here!'

They collided moments later in an ecstatic flurry of kisses and hugs. Presently Simon greeted Pippa over Sally's shoulder as she continued to crush him in a tight embrace.

'Hugo said to say sorry, Pippa, but he'll be along shortly. He's just tied up with something.'

Or more likely, someone, thought Pippa.

At last the initial emotional onslaught subsided, allowing Simon leisure to look around him.

'Well, this is nice. I don't think I've been in here before. Very pleasant indeed. Good choice. So, what will you girls have?'

His eye suddenly fell on the large screen permanently tuned to Sky Sports.

'Oh look, they're previewing the match. Look at that - wasn't that a wonderful goal! Great move! Lampard's such a fantastic player! I think if Chelsea can reproduce that kind of form…'

'Filthy! Dirty! Perversion! How dare you do that in public!'

Simon spun round.

'What? I…'

'That disgusting, disgusting activity! Horrible, violent, disgusting rubbish! How could you? You of all people! How could you do this to me!'

'Sally, I…'

She cut him off with a wild, aggrieved gesture.

'I'm going, and I don't want to see or hear from you again! Ever!'

Sally slammed out of the pub, and there followed a long, shocked silence. Simon swayed uncertainly, as if he'd just been caught a glancing blow from a 40-ton truck. Finally he turned to Pippa with wide, staring eyes.

'What happened?'

Pippa sighed and shook her head.

'No - I mean it - what happened? One minute she was all over me, then the very next second she goes berserk. I didn't know she was a psychopath.'

'She's not a psychopath, Simon. She's just a woman. And we all have our little ups and downs. And unfortunately you managed to push all the wrong buttons all at the same time. In fact, you couldn't have done the job more effectively if you'd planned and coordinated it. Why on earth did you have to draw attention to the football?'

'How was I to know she doesn't like football, for God's sake?'

'Simon, I think you really need to come to terms with the gravity of your offence.'

'What offence? I haven't done anything!'

'You've offended Sally to the very core of her being. Did you really not know how much she despises football?'

'No, of course not. The subject has never come up.'

'That's unfortunate - I wish I'd known beforehand. Still, it's too late now. All we can hope for now is a repair job.'

'What the hell is all this about? Why does she hate it so much?'

'Simon, you might have noticed that Sally has very strong opinions and a highly developed but idiosyncratic worldview?'

'I had noticed. It's one of the many things that attracted me to her in the first place.'

'Well, that's good, and in many ways it's a very positive force. Unfortunately, however, it means that she feels it necessary to take a stand against those things which don't fit into this worldview. And one of the things she dislikes more than anything else is that peculiarly violent, uncivilized and generally disgusting activity masquerading as sport which she regards, not unreasonably, as a hotbed for all the thugs, morons, fanatics, nationalists, jingoists and tribalists who make up the detritus of society.'

'By which you mean football, I suppose?'

'You're catching on.'

'You sound as if you agree with her.'

'I'm just trying to demonstrate the strength of her feelings. So when you made those light-hearted and ostensibly harmless comments, it was quite simply the worst thing that you could possibly have done.

Apart from come in here dressed up as a soldier, carrying a rifle.'

'What?'

'Never mind. Another time, maybe. Simon, I'm going after Sally. I'll try to reason with her. Stay here and wait for Hugo, will you?'

'He's here now, Pippa.'

She looked across to where Hugo approached, his expression sombre. They passed, pausing only briefly for the slightest of exchanges.

12

Pippa tentatively pushed open the door to Sally's office. Sally sat alone, head bowed. She momentarily turned a heart-wrenching look towards Pippa, then snatched up a pen and made a show of looking at some papers on her desk. Pippa regarded her friend with kind eyes.

'Hello, Sally.'

No response.

'Where's Jemima?' she said softly.

This time Sally looked up, her expression distraught though her voice remained steady.

'Repainting her face. Or the Forth Bridge, I forget which. Something, at any rate, which never quite actually reaches a conclusion.'

'Sally, we have to talk.'

'Well I don't. Anyway, conversation is considerably overrated. It's what people do when they've run out of things to say.'

'I know you're upset.'

'Upset? Me? Why should I be upset that I appear to be the only person in the world with the wit to understand anything I say? I should regard it as a compliment. In fact, I probably would, had I the least respect for the intellect of those paying it.'

'Sally, darling.'

For all her brave words Sally now appeared, for once, to be on the brink of tears.

'I thought he was special,' she said, haltingly. 'I thought he was the one.'

'He is the one, the one for you.'

'No he isn't! How can he be now?'

'Sally, nothing's changed. Simon is still the same person he was yesterday, and the day before that. And so are you. Nothing has changed except your perception of him. And that's something entirely within your control.'

'Nothing has changed except that I now think he's an unreconstructed idiot. And that because he is one, he'll now think that I'm just some crazy fanatic.'

'Darling, Simon wouldn't want you to moderate your views, or temper your sensibilities. It is precisely your big emotions and big ideas that he loves, I'm sure. But you have to allow just a little leeway for the frailties and failings of others. Not everyone can match up to your shining ideals, darling. And that doesn't necessarily make Simon an idiot.'

'But he clearly hasn't understood a single word I've been saying! He wouldn't have come out with such unthinking comments about something I hate so much if he did understand me. How can I love him now?'

'Sally, darling, you know you love him. Just because he doesn't in every way reflect your worldview just now, give him time. As soon as he's aware of the minutiae of your philosophy, I'm sure his thinking will mature very swiftly, and along very similar lines. You've had your entire life to reach the point you are now. And, who knows, you may develop further yet.'

'If I do have the good fortune to develop further yet, you can be sure that any development will exclude that deviant perversion known as football.'

Pippa laughed, and tried to hug Sally, who acquiesced briefly, before shrugging her off.

'Darling, you can't expect someone to share every aspect of your vision. It's unique to you. It's your vision.'

'But the man I love must agree with me in everything, Pippa. I mean our ideas must agree in everything. Our ideas, our thoughts, our emotions - all must be as one in a true coming together of our souls.'

'Sally, that's nonsense. You are complete and wonderful in yourself. Better by far that both of you are strong and individual in your own right, and respect each other's differences.'

'But that's the trouble, Pippa. I can't respect someone who likes football! And if I can't respect them I can't love them. I can't even like them! In fact I would have to hate, despise and loathe them with every fibre of my being!'

'My dear Sally, I think you're finally ready for the easy give and take of marriage, that ready compromise and generous forbearance of each other's quirks and foibles that underpins that blissful state!'

'Don't make fun of me, Pippa.'

'I wasn't really, darling. Look Sally, you have to let Simon deal with these issues in his own way. You cannot set him on a pedestal as an ideal of perfection, and then reject him if he so much as wobbles.'

'He never deserved to be on the pedestal in the first place.'

'Darling, as long as you are true to yourself, and inviolate in yourself, then surely you can be tolerant of weakness in others? None of us are perfect, Sally. None of us are wholly good. All of us have dark, violent or perverse thoughts from time to time. All of us, Sally - perhaps even you. To be civilized is to contain the primitive within us and act in the way we would wish to do - not to pretend this darker side doesn't exist. In a social sense, you could say that life is a continuous process of overcoming one's natural inclinations.'

'I never thought to hear such a puritan philosophy from you, Pippa.'

'I didn't mean it in a repressive or restrictive way. Look Sally, Herland is fiction. I think it has become too much of an ideal in your mind. And that now you reject anything that doesn't measure up to its peerless purity. Let Simon have his football, darling. I know it offends you, but try to be tolerant and forgiving.'

'I can't! I can't compromise! I need society to be as it is in Herland, where aggression and violence in any form are simply unthinkable - not even taboo, but simply not a part of consciousness. There are times in the book when the captive men relate details of their life back home - events they regard as unavoidable, everyday commonplaces - and the women are often shocked and revolted, though out of courtesy they do their best to hide it. They feel violated simply by the relation of these horrors - to them unthinkable images going into their minds.'

'Darling, I understand what you're saying. But a lot of people think football is just a harmless pastime. But anyway,' Pippa continued hurriedly, 'what about something fairly innocuous like Sherlock Holmes, or Poirot, which obviously rely on the depiction of violence and criminal actions for the entire functioning of the plot? Would you really want to - '

'Of course I would, if it contributed to an unhealthy societal state of mind. But even in some silly detective drama the violence doesn't have to be explicit, or indeed seen at all. It can simply be referred to obliquely if it's absolutely necessary to explain the plot.'

'I think it probably would be necessary, darling, in a detective story.'

'Why this endless obsession with violence? Why can't we move on, and leave such primitivism behind? Anyway, the existence of such stuff isn't important. If such rubbish is still in print at all in two, three hundred years' time - which I fervently hope is not the case - it will be viewed by civilized beings of the future simply as an anthropological curiosity, and therefore with complete detachment. As, in fact, one would view the behaviour of any species in the wild. The women of Herland had no respect for the past or its ideas - Why should we, they argued, when our forebears knew so much less than we do? And the same will apply to us if we actually manage to progress and mature. Don't you see, Pippa - I want the human race to move towards what it has the potential to be. I can't simply write it off - not yet, anyway. I don't feel quite old enough for the gentle balm of committed cynicism. And it's not because humanity is something wonderful at this moment - quite the reverse.'

'Darling, you have to live in the real world, to some extent.'

'There is no real world. The only real world is the one in my head. That is the only real one as far as I'm concerned. And I object to savages invading and polluting it.'

'Sally, you just have to stop them getting inside your head. I know you want and must keep to the purity of your ideals, but you can't stop things happening, and of you being aware of them. But you do have the choice as to whether they get inside your mind or not.'

'I can't! I can't stop them! That's the trouble. How do I ignore it, how do I keep the purity of myself, without cutting myself off from humanity, with all its crudity and violence?'

'Darling, you can't stop people being savages. It just isn't possible. But you can control whether you let it get to you or not.'

'It's your fault! You're the commissioning editor. Why do you keep promoting the violent rubbish Minty and Freddy like? How do you prevent these images polluting your mind when you, of all people, are complicit in promoting this garbage?'

'That's not fair, Sally. You know full well that Freddy has promised to raise the standard of what we publish, and to moderate the material where necessary - very much, I think, thanks to the power of your arguments. That's an extraordinary compliment to you personally, and to your powers of dialectic and persuasion. But also, please remember that my authority in this firm is strictly limited. Commissioning editor is just a title, and it doesn't really mean very much. It's Freddy's show. He might seem to take a back seat much of the time, but in the final analysis it's he who sets the agenda here, not me.'

'I am already diminished! Every violent act I have ever seen in reality or on TV, or read of in books or seen in films has polluted my brain, and diminished me. That's why I resent so much any attempt to pollute and diminish me further. What right has some deranged writer or filmmaker to off-load their disgusting perversions on me?'

'Darling, I know how much it hurt you when Simon showed an interest in the football on TV.'

'Football!'

Hatred and contempt in her voice.

'Look Sally, just say to yourself, Yes, I know there are savages, and I know they do savage, brutal things. And my power to affect such things is very limited. But they are in a minority. And they cannot change what is pure and inviolate in me unless I let them. What is inviolable can never be violated. You spoke about Herland just now. Do you remember the part where the narrator, Vandyck Jennings, is telling Ellador about the concept of predestination and damnation, and how this necessarily applied even to infants?'

'Yes, of course. What of it?'

'You remember her reaction to this? How she went running to the nearest temple to receive consolation from a wise woman?'

Sally nodded.

'The woman told her that the concept never had any meaning. That people who are stupid and ignorant will believe anything. Sally, you give these events, these thoughts about violence, power by attaching meaning to them. They are the actions of wild, ignorant and uncivilized creatures just as surely as any beast of the jungle or plain. You know all this yourself, Sally. What is born of ignorance has no meaning or significance. It might be unpleasant, shocking even, but it has no meaning unless you sanction it by attaching meaning to it. It can't touch or hurt you, Sally, if you perceive it to be no more brutal or offensive than the lion sinking its teeth into the neck of the zebra. Human violence is no more offensive than that, if you realise that it's the result of pure ignorance - nothing more or less. And therefore it has no connection or relevance to you, or any civilized person. There are many gradations of the human race, and some are closer to our animal neighbours than others. Such that sometimes they can be viewed almost as a separate species. And of course some, like Simon, require only education and a gentle, guiding hand to join the swelling ranks of civilized humanity.'

'Pippa,' said Sally, throwing her arms around her, hugging her tightly and crying with emotion, 'you are beautiful and wise! And I love you! You are the only person who bothers to understand me. Thank you so much! I love you!'

'Darling, show Simon what he means to you. Express your real feelings to him. Don't risk losing the wonderful thing that you have between you. Go to him, Sally! Go to him now, darling!'

13

Simon left Hugo after twenty minutes or so, Hugo preferring to be alone to indulge the sharp edges of his sorrow. Now Simon sat at his desk, deep in perplexing sorrow of his own.

The office door slowly opened, just sufficiently for the striking, elevated cheekbones of Laraine to make an entrance.

'Is Hugo here?'

A theatrical whisper. Simon glanced around the empty office.

'Clearly not.'

'Good. Because it's you I want to see.'

Simon maintained a defensive position behind his desk as Laraine stepped in, closing the door behind her.

'Why? What do you want with me? I haven't done anything.'

She leaned over the desk towards him.

'I like you! What's your name?'

'I don't know. I mean, I haven't got a name.'

She reached out and brushed her hand across his cheek.

'You're Simon, aren't you.'

'No. Oh yes, alright, I'm Simon. If you know, why ask?'

'You know, you're kinda cute!'

'No, I'm not.'

'Not pretty exactly, but just nice and compact and built in all the right places. Know what I mean?'

'No, I don't know what you mean at all. And it's clearly time you left.'

She laughed, and walked over to the window and looked out.

'What an awful sterile environment!'

'I know. I've often said so. There's nothing I can do about it, I'm afraid.'

'But I'll bet it's not sterile in here.'

'Oh, but it is. Appallingly so. Would that it were not, but there we are.'

'Not with you here, Simon. And when Hugo's here too, the room must just buzz with masculine potency.'

Simon looked hard at her.

'It's you, isn't it.'

'What's me, honey? Oh, that look of English indignation is so funny, but cute too! I love impotent anger! It brings out all my protective instincts. Come here, Simon - you need a hug!'

'It's you sending Hugo those texts, isn't it?'

Laraine laughed.

'What texts are those, honey?'

'You know very well what I'm talking about.'

'Why in the world would I send Hugo texts when I can call in here to see you boys just whenever I want?'

'You're stalking him.'

She laughed again, tossing back her head in an extraordinary, abandoned gesture.

'Do you realise the trouble you've caused? The suffering - both to Hugo and his wife?'

She was still smiling.

'Well, do you?'

She sat down at Hugo's desk, reaching forward for the Newton's Cradle which Hugo kept beside his model of a Porsche. She took a shiny silver ball bearing at each end of the toy in the fingers of each hand. Then began banging the ball bearings inward simultaneously with a succession of sharp, rhythmical clicks. Simon watched in fascination and distaste at such horribly impressive self-possession. The clicking continued interminably, Laraine's expression one of hypnotic, smiling concentration.

At last she released her hold on the ball bearings, and watched them as they continued to dangle limply.

'You know, I try not to think about Hugo too much. But he is such a big, big boy!'

'Yes, he is a big boy, but that's really not the point. He's married. You shouldn't have done it. It wasn't nice, and it's put a big strain on his marriage.'

'Well,' she said, looking up at Simon, 'never mind, honey.'

He frowned.

'What do you mean, never mind? Do you really not care about the damage you've caused? You know there are laws in this country specifically aimed at people like you.'

She rose to her feet, and giving the ball bearings one last, gentle tap with one finger that sent them swinging helplessly once more, walked over towards the door.

'Look,' said Simon, struggling to maintain his composure, 'I'll make you a deal. And this is a one-off, one-time offer. If you promise to stop sending any more texts - in fact promise not to initiate any kind of contact with Hugo outside of work - then I'll keep this matter between ourselves. But one more text - and I mean just the one - and Hugo will know, the top brass will hear of it and the police will be informed.'

He was taking deep, nervous breaths. This sort of situation wasn't his normal beat. And time had almost ceased to pass before her ice-blue eyes met his in mocking salute, and the corners of her wide lips crinkled in appreciation.

'I really like you, Simon! But honey, I only called by to tell Hugo I'm going back to New York.'

'New York?'

'Don't look so disappointed, doll! Look me up if you can get over - I'd like to see much more of you! Oh, and give my love to Hugo, won't you? Tell him I'll miss him.'

The door closed behind her.

Two minutes later it opened again. Hugo appeared, looking haggard and unkempt.

'I thought I saw Laraine just now.'

'I know.'

'How do you know?'

'I mean, did you?'

'Has she been here?'

'Who?'

'What's going on, Simon?'

'I can't say anything. What I mean to say is, there is nothing to say.'

'So she was here?'

'I've got something rather wonderful to tell you, Hugo. Although I can't say too much because I'm sworn to secrecy.'

'It'll be the first wonderful thing I've heard today.'

'All your worries are at an end.'
'All of them?'
'I mean the particular worry that's been worrying you so much lately.'
'So it was her.'
'No more unwanted texts.'
'I should have guessed.'
'No more stalking.'
'That woman really is the limit.'
'No more harassment.'
'The gall of the creature!'
'However, there is one condition, upon which I'm afraid I must insist.'
'What's that?'
'I'm not at liberty to tell you who this person is. I gave her - or him - my word - my solemn promise - that I would reveal her - or his - identity to nobody. And that of course includes you, Hugo.'
'Well, don't tell me then.'
'Don't worry, I won't.'
'So she was here, then.'
'Who?'
'Laraine.'
'It was either her or someone impersonating her.'
'Is that likely?'
'Both are equally likely and yet equally unlikely.'
'How singular.'

'You know what you must do now, don't you, Hugo?'

'What?'

'Go to her. I mean go to Pippa. Go to her and tell her the truth, the whole truth and whatever minor details you consider it safe to reveal.'

'I'll tell her everything. I have nothing to hide.'

'The man with nothing to hide is one of life's eternal passengers; a man with a season ticket but no destination.'

'I am forever in your debt, Simon.'

'Think nothing of it, Hugo. No more than you deserve. Now go, and Godspeed!'

The door closed behind him.

Two minutes later it opened again. This time it was Sally, her expression sombre, her face tear-stained. She made no move to approach Simon, but gazed deeply, longingly into his eyes. He got up, and stood with his back to the window. And still they faced each other silently. Then Simon began to recite, slowly, caressingly, his voice soft, low and musical.

> *'Your eyes as stars of twilight fair,*
> *Like twilight's, too, your dusky hair,*
> *But all things else about you drawn,*
> *From May-time and the cheerful dawn.'*

Sally could contain herself no longer. She flung herself into Simon's arms. She sobbed, and her tears flowed. Amid her tears, Simon whispered softly, finding words that found their mark in Sally's heart.

> *'One word is too often profaned*
> *For me to profane it;*
> *One feeling too falsely disdain'd*
> *For thee to disdain it;*
> *I can give not what men call love:*
> *But wilt thou accept not*
> *The worship the heart lifts above*
> *And the Heavens reject not,*
> *The desire of the moth for the star,*
> *Of the night for the morrow,*
> *The devotion to something afar*
> *From the sphere of our sorrow?'*

'Oh, my love! My dear, dear love!'

'Darling Sally!'

'Simon, can I have faith in what you say? Does the fire in your heart match the lustre of your words?'

'My sweet darling, can you doubt it?'

'Oh, my dear and beautiful Simon! Those wonderful words - did you make them up yourself, my sweet?'

'Almost entirely, my love!'

'Oh, my wonderful and inspired darling!'

'My dearest sweet, there remains one matter still standing between us.'

'How can that be, my sweetest angel?'

'It is a subject that I hesitate to broach.'

'Broach it, my dearest love! Have no fear!'

'In that case, my dearest Sally,' whispering ever more gently in her ear, 'can I be completely forthright with you?'

Sally closed her eyes and swallowed hard.

'It would give me much, much pleasure were you to be so.'

'Well, my love, I want to tell you that I hate football. I have always hated it. In fact I regard it as little more or less than a deviant perversion. I only ever pretended to take an interest in it to fit in with everybody else.'

'Is all this true, Simon?'

She pulled back slightly, her dazzling blue eyes wide and hopeful, running her fingers through his nondescript hair.

'No, but if you would only believe me, darling, it would mean so much to me - to both of us.'

Sally's eyes filled with tears, and she hugged Simon closer still.

'Of course I believe you, my love, if that is what you wish. In fact, my darling, when you speak with so much sincerity, I tend to believe almost anything you say. Especially something I am already predetermined to believe.'

'Oh my darling! I'm so pleased we're both predetermined to believe in much the same things at last!'

'And no doubt disbelieve with equal determination in much the same things, and with almost equal facility.'

'Oh Sally, your words give me a sense of almost equal felicity!'

'I'm sorry to have to point this out, my dear love, but you seem a little confused. I actually said facility.'

'No matter, my lovely darling! The way I feel at the moment, the precise spelling of a word is inconsequential, as is its meaning.'

'Oh, my darling!'

'My sweet love!'

'But you do really hate it now, my dear one, don't you?'

'Hate what, my little darling?'

'That perversion whose name I cannot bring myself to mention.'

'Oh, you mean football? Yes, oh yes, of course, my dear love, yes of course I do.'

'I knew it would be so! I love you so much, my dear and wonderful Simon! Now everything is perfect between us, and shall remain forever so!'

'Yes, my dear little darling! Until the event of our next slight divergence of opinion, everything shall remain forever perfect between us.'

They embrace passionately once more, showering each other with kisses. While beyond the opaque window of Simon's office the scene remains one of absolute sterility, inside the office big emotions are the order of the day.

'Oh, Hugo! I have been a fool to doubt you! How can you ever forgive me? How can I ever forgive myself?'

Pippa's body quivered in his strong arms.

'My darling, there is nothing to forgive. There is only our own reticence to condemn, our own failure to adequately express those feelings that we both so strongly feel.'

'You are so, so right, my angel. And so it was another all along.'

'Another, yes. But another that was to me, as much as to you, a stranger, in any sense that has meaning.'

'Except, of course, in the sense that you did, in fact, know her.'

'Yes, my darling, except, of course, in that sense. But clearly I did not, in fact, really know her, in any sense that would impart meaning to this whole unfortunate episode.'

'Or expiation.'

'My love, there is nothing for either of us to expiate. Apart, of course, from the failure to adequately express what has always been deepest in both our hearts.'

'As Sally has always said.'

'As Sally, as you quite rightly say, my love, has always said.'

'Oh, Hugo!'

'Oh, Pippa!'

14

In the magical, scented balm of early evening, Sally caught sight of Araminta standing at the far end of Freddy's balustraded, stone-flagged terrace. She was gazing speculatively over the rolling acres encompassing paddocks (with windbreaker), ornamental ponds and formal mature gardens, and her well-conditioned hair was moving gently in the soft, consoling breeze. Sally calls to her. Araminta turns, smiles and goes over to meet her. They hug.

'Sally, you're wearing perfume! It's lovely! What is it?'

'Oh, it's not really a proper perfume, just something I got from Superdrug. Kylie Sweet Darling Eau de Toilette. It's not as good as yours, of course.'

'I think it's lovely!'

'Thanks, Araminta! By the way, your hair is wonderfully shiny tonight! What conditioner do you use?'

'Oh, it's just Farrell's Daily Conditioner. I have it specially imported from the States. It contains whole wheat protein and natural botanical extracts.

I think it really adds tensile strength, as well as restoring moisture and sealing the cuticle layer.'

'Wow! All that, plus it looks so good!'

'Hello, Araminta!'

'Oh, hello Simon. I didn't see you there standing next to Sally.'

Simon quickly rallied.

'You're looking very beautiful tonight, Araminta!'

'That's kind of you, Simon. Well, of course it is a special occasion, so I did go to some lengths with my hair and make-up.'

'Your make-up is wonderful,' said Sally. 'It's beautifully understated.'

'Oh thanks, Sally! But aren't you wearing just a touch of eye shadow and eyeliner yourself?'

'Well, just a little. Of course, I'm no expert, unlike you, so I kept it to a minimum.'

'But it works so much better like that! You've done a wonderful job, Sally! I think that's another area in which I can learn so much from you!'

There was a call and wave from Freddy at the door leading out to the terrace.

'Quickly, everyone! Pippa and Hugo want to make an announcement!'

There followed a hurried transfer into the medieval-style reception room, where Simon, Sally and Araminta joined the others already assembled around the fireplace. Champagne appeared and found its way into eager hands.

'We just couldn't wait any longer, could we, my love?'

Pippa's eyes were sparkling.

'No, my love, it appears that we couldn't.'

'Darling, it's really perfectly natural. Well, everyone, Hugo and I want to tell you that - we're having a baby!'

A chorus of congratulations and excited inquiry. Freddy proposed an appropriate toast.

'There's just one thing worrying me,' said Hugo.

'I think I understand,' said Simon. 'But you know, Hugo, as Pippa says, it really is quite natural.'

'No, it's not that.'

'Oh, you mean the other thing? Well, I've had a thought about that too.'

'You have?'

'Certainly. Porsche Cayenne.'

'Mm. Bit of a van, isn't it?'

'God, man, you really search out the dark lining, don't you. It is still a Porsche, Hugo.'

'I know, I know, but…'

'Well?'

'Would such a thing really have been driven by the Stig? Realistically?'

Simon moved to Hugo's side and laid a gentle hand on his forearm.

'Hugo, I'm not entirely sure. But given your situation - a growing family - sorry, Hugo, I expressed it as delicately as possible - and the hostile situation in Hampstead and so on - I'm sure the Stig would understand and sanction the compromise necessary in running a 4x4, even if, and for that very reason, he's avoided it like the plague.'

Hugo thanked Simon warmly.

'In fact, we've got a little announcement of our own to make,' said Freddy.

Everyone turned to Freddy, Araminta close beside him, her eyes and hair shining.

'Well, the thing is that we, that is Araminta and I, are engaged!'

'To be married!' said Araminta in eager confirmation, her eyes captivated by the generous proportions of the reception room.

Another chorus of congratulations and excited inquiry, Hugo this time proposing the appropriate toast.

'Well, not to be left out,' said Daniel, 'in fact we've got our own little announcement to make.'

All eyes turned to Daniel, Jemima close beside him, looking up admiringly.

'I and Jemima, I mean Jemima and I, and me - well, the thing is, we're engaged too!'

'To be married too!' confirmed Jemima, with only a hint of a sniff.

Another chorus of congratulations and excited inquiry, Pippa fielding the appropriate toast this time.

'Well, this is all quite remarkable,' said Sally. 'And so as not to spoil the extraordinary symmetry of the proceedings, we've got a couple of announcements to make too.'

All eyes turned to Sally, Simon standing close beside her.

'Well, as you might have guessed by now, there obviously being something in the air in this particular part of the Surrey countryside, we, too, are engaged!'

'And we also anticipate that it will in due course result in marriage,' said Simon.

Another chorus of congratulations and excited inquiry.

'To Sally and S - '

'Hang on, there's something else I want to announce first.'

All eyes turned specifically to Sally.

'I want to tell you all, that I'm declaring war on male violence and aggression.'

'That's wonderful, darling! said Pippa. 'And what precise form will this war take?'

'I'm starting a new political movement. It's called WAVE.'

'Wave?' said Simon.

'Women Against Violence. WAVE. What has always annoyed me more than most things is that people accept violence as an unavoidable part of human experience. It isn't. By and large, it's what silly boys do when they're left to their own devices, simply because they haven't been taught any better. That's why they mustn't be left to their own devices. And that's why I'm founding WAVE.'

'What a wonderful idea, Sally!'

'You are wonderful!'

'Quite remarkable!'

'WAVE will make it impossible for any silly boy ever again to pick up a rifle, or put on a uniform, or for any silly girl to accept this as normal. No more unthinking obedience, no authority, no violence, no dogmatism. Silly boys waving guns around historically create problems that other silly boys with guns then heroically solve. And silly girls alternately suffer and cheer from the sidelines. It's just some ludicrous self-perpetuating game, born out of ignorance and stupidity. Two things that historically, as I'm sure you're all well aware by now, annoy the fuck out of me. WAVE will render all such nonsense completely obsolete.'

'You mean, I suppose,' said Simon, 'that national armies will be subsumed within an international peacekeeping force resulting in the complete demilitarisation of all aligned states.'

Sally hesitated.

'Certainly.'

'Extraordinary!'

'You are marvellous, Sally!'

'WAVE will challenge and overturn all the tired and tiresome assumptions about gender differences. It's just men doing men things and boys doing boy things. And they can't help it, so let's all have a giggle! Oh, he's a man, he can't help it! Well, of course, we can multitask and they can't! Men! FUCK-WITS! How stupid do you have to be to qualify as Fuck-wit of the Year? How many fuck-wits DOES it take to change a light bulb?'

'Fantastic!'

'Oh Sally!'

'Herland challenges and dismantles the notion of society based on gender differences. And WAVE will continue Gilman's work to its logical conclusion.'

'Wonderful!'

'WAVE will call on all men everywhere to lay down their arms and take off their uniforms.'

'Fabulous!'

'Just imagine, if every man in every army refused to fight, refused to carry a weapon, refused to carry out orders, there would be no more war! Ever! It's so, so simple! And all women have to do is refuse to sleep with any man who engages in any form of violent activity or wears a uniform or carries a weapon.'

'Ah,' smiled Simon. 'Shades of Lysistrata!'

Sally regarded him blankly.

'Sorry, carry on.'

'All such mindless perverts must be disowned by society, and women in particular. I can't see the struggle lasting too long if we stick to our guns.'

'Certainly not,' said Simon. 'It should all be over by Christmas.'

'You've done it again, darling!'

'But can men join WAVE?' asked Simon. 'I'd really like to.'

'Yes, of course,' said Sally, 'so long as they embrace its whole ethos and adhere strictly to feminine values.'

'Sounds good to me,' said Simon.

'And me,' said Freddy.

'Me too,' said Hugo.

'And as more and more people join WAVE, and its shining philosophy becomes ever more universally adopted, the savages will become more and more marginalized. Until eventually, like the

Neanderthals, they will die out completely. And to hasten this process, and because of the vital importance of the need to exercise extreme care in the shaping of young minds, WAVE will campaign for violent scenes to be cut out of all books, films, cartoons and playstation games. Only those products that satisfy exacting WAVE criteria will receive the official WAVE stamp of approval and carry the official WAVE logo.'

'But wouldn't that make some books and films rather incomprehensible?' asked Pippa tentatively.

The company drew in a collective, expectant breath.

'Pippa, true art is never, nor intended to be, comprehensible. The wonder and mystery of existence is beyond explanation, and what is art if not the summation and distillation of that mystery, the miracle of pure sensation. The man who seeks the explicable is the man who has renounced his soul.'

'But what is the soul?' asked Araminta.

'The soul is the world through the eyes of a cat - without judgement or pity, without thought, analysis or intellect, the indivisible, inexplicable core of self - pure existence, pure essence, pure abstraction.'

'But what is existence?' asked Hugo.

'Existence is the candle in the dead of night, a footprint in the sand, the shadow of the clouds on the mountain top.'

'But what is essence?' asked Jemima.

'Art is pure essence, and the essence of pure art is that inexplicable core of abstraction. All art is distillation, and all distillation is pure art.'

'But what is abstraction?' asked Daniel.

'Abstraction is the distillation of art - the pure art that expresses the distilled essence of pure sensation.'

'But what is sensation?' asked Freddy.

'Sensation is the whisper of the artist's dream, the intensity of abstraction, the distillation of emotion. And the expression of pure emotion shall always remain the highest, purest form of art.'

At first a hushed silence, then -
    'Sally...'
    'Sally, darling!'
    'Sally, you are wonderful!'
    'Oh Sally!'
    'It's all down to you, Sally,' said Pippa, quietly and reverently. 'Thank you! Thank you for everything! If you hadn't shown us how to express our emotions, who knows what might have become of us.'

'I'd like to second that, Pippa,' said Hugo, his glorious features suffused with warm admiration. 'Without you, Sally, the future would have been very different - very different indeed. In fact, it hardly bears thinking about.'

'That goes for me too, Sally,' said Araminta, her smile sweet and sincere. 'As you say, Hugo, it hardly bears thinking about. We all owe you so much, Sally.'

'I've always had great faith in your wisdom and judgement, Sally,' said Freddy, genially. 'You've taught us all so much.'

'Especially about emotions,' said Daniel, one arm around Jemima's waist.

'And the need to express them,' said Jemima, smiling shyly up at him.

They all raise their glasses.

'To Sally - thinker, wit and muse to all true artists everywhere!'

'And to Simon, the only man who could possibly have captured her heart!'

'To Sally and Simon!'

'To Sally and Simon!'

'To us all!'

'To us all!'

'And to emotions!'

'To emotions!'

Of course, it's customary for the toasts to be made after rather than before a meal. But the unconventional approach adopted here works rather better for our purposes. As it means that now we can leave our friends in peace to enjoy their dinner, safe from further prying or comment.

And in any case, as you must be aware by now, from the telltale compression of my spinal column due to long hours at my writing desk composing this short narrative, all has been hastening swiftly towards a condition of felicitous complacency. And so, gentle reader, let me in conclusion, while wishing to avoid sententious moralising, offer this reflection. Let there be no subduing of passions or emotions, for they are the best, as well as the worst of us, and lead us to the high, as well as to the low ground. Let us take what they have to offer, and make of them what we may. And let there be no settling, let there be no humble regrets. Let us accept, nay embrace, our emotions and say, This is what it is to be human! And let the man who has cast the first stone furthest reap the richest harvest, for only the sheep that follow the wolf will gather the whirlwind.

Printed in Great Britain
by Amazon